MASTER

MEN OF CLUB TRISKELION

J.L. QUICK

AUTHOR'S NOTE

This novel is a contemporary dark romance. It contains scenes and descriptive adult content, recommended for adult (18+) readers.

As a contemporary, dark romance work of fiction, this novel is not intended to be a portrayal of a healthy relationship or a 'how to guide' for the kink and lifestyle elements depicted within.

For those interested in exploring aspects of kink and/or dominant-submissive relationships explored in the following chapters, please do so responsibly and with appropriate reference materials.

TRIGGER WARNINGS

This novel may contain scenes and descriptive adult content that might be triggering for some readers.

GLOSSARY

This novel contains dialect commonly found in Ireland and Great Britain.

Brigadier—Bratva captain

Go hálainn—beautiful

Kryshas—brutal Bratva enforcer

Lad—young man

Malen'kaya printsessa—little princess

Manky—dirty, disgusting, rotten

Mo chéadsearc—my first love

Mo chuisle—my pulse/my darling

Mo ghrá—my love

Mo mhuirnín—my sweetheart

Piscín—kitten

Plonker—fool

Póg mo thóin—kiss my ass

Sashenka—little Sasha

Taibhseach—gorgeous

Uncail—uncle

Wank/wanking off—masturbating

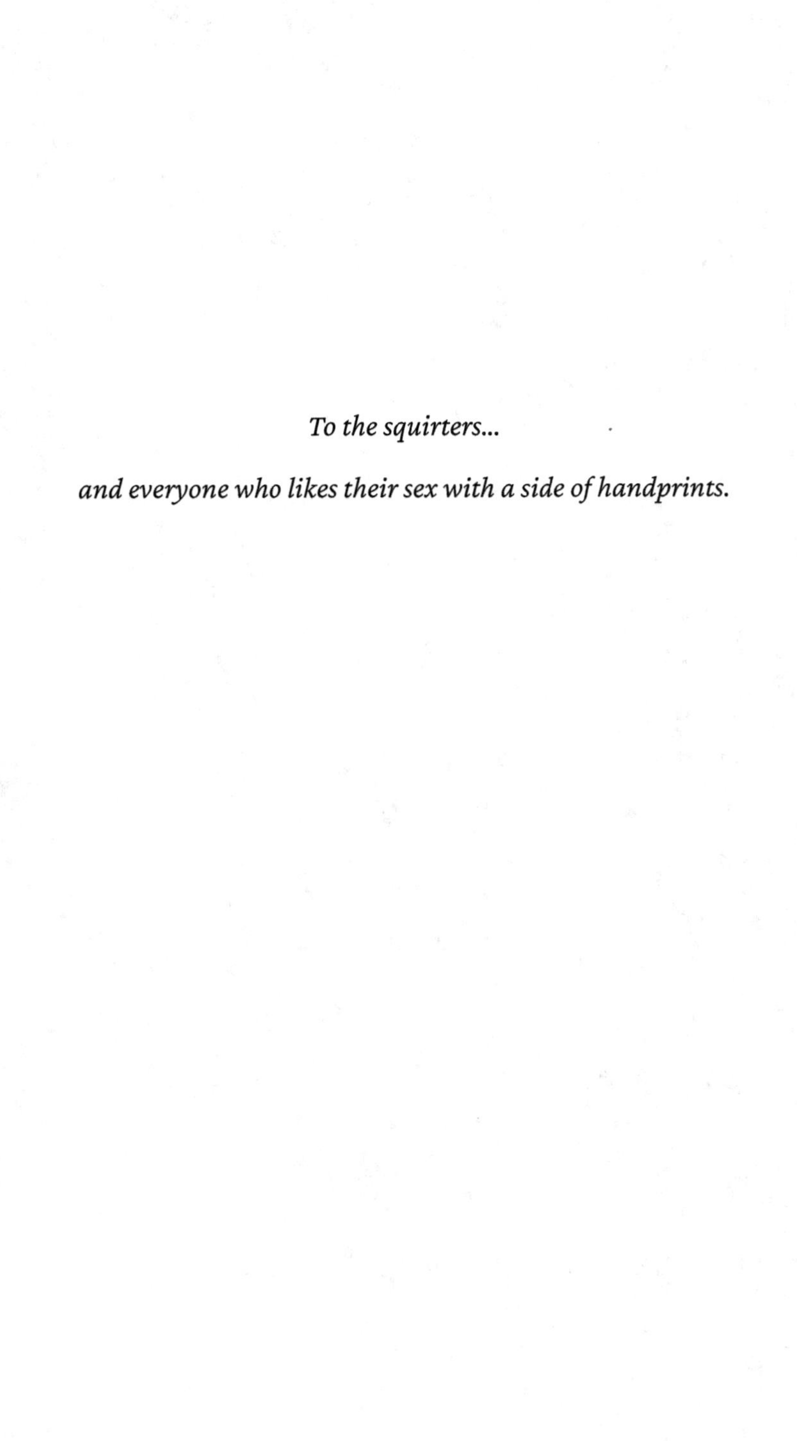

To the squirters...

and everyone who likes their sex with a side of handprints.

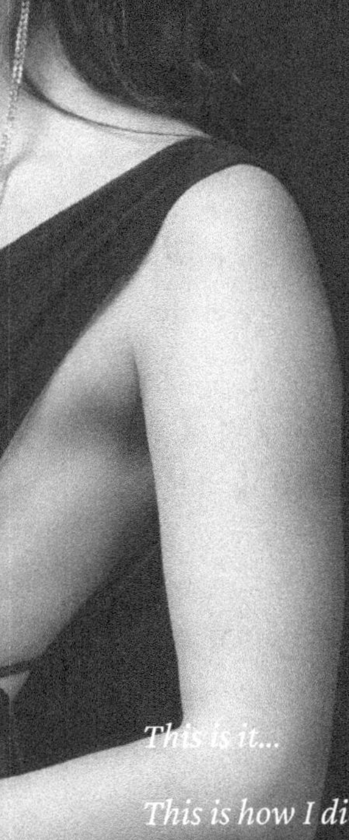

CHAPTER ONE
SASHA

This is it...

This is how I die...

Bound, gagged, and with a sea of people watching.

My sweat pools on the black leather my stomach is firmly pressed against. The cushion quickly growing slick from the puddle of adrenaline seeping through my skin. I slide through the slippery wetness as I try futilely to retreat from the brutal strikes Isaac continues to land across my ass and thighs. My forearms and shins are tied so tightly to the spanking bench that my mobility is limited to a few inches at most.

This is how Isaac likes me: bound and silently enduring my grueling punishment.

All the Doms that I have been with were cruel on occasion, but Isaac isn't like any of them.

He's worse.

With him, there is no difference between playtime and punishment. Both are focused on inflicting as much pain as I can endure. Sometimes more. Neither involves pleasure—*well, at least not usually mine.*

Isaac gets off on my suffering; both physical and mental. He shares me with his friends—letting them watch him fuck me or dictate how I please myself—only to then spend days denying and berating me as a punishment for being a whore. The pain of denial and humiliation from his degradation is easy to endure compared to his physical impact play and sadism. He isn't satisfied until he has left his mark in the form of bruises, welts, or blood. Or, from the roughest of our times together, all the above.

Like a good submissive, I give him everything he wants. No matter how hard it is to take it. When he's satisfied with pushing me to the brink of unconsciousness—sometimes further—he claims me and says the words that make it all worth it. *"You're mine. No one will ever want you the way I do."*

Taking every hurtful word, denied orgasm, stranger's eyes on me, and pained strike without complaint makes me good enough. *Wanted.* Worthy of being *his* submissive.

With each breath harder than the last, I struggle to suck in air through my restraints and the pain he's inflicting to put on a show for our audience. I remind myself through every short, labored breath, *"It'll be worth it, Sasha."* The heavy wooden paddle Isaac has been using hits my ass again, and the thuddy sting radiates across my skin as tears well in my eyes. He swings again and hits a tender, overly-struck section of my upper thigh. The pain sears along my backside, and I cry out, but my scream is muffled by the inflated butterfly gag occupying my mouth.

I shouldn't have told him I didn't want to do this exhibition.

Isaac swings again and again. The cumulative pain becomes unbearable, and I press my forehead to the leather beneath me in an attempt to hide the tears currently streaming down my cheeks. My heart stops when the soles of his shoes click against the black marble floors, and his fingers trail up the length of my spine.

"Look at me," he snarls from above. Sucking in a small snot-filled breath, I lift my face from the sticky leather and open my eyes. His fingers lace through my sweat-matted hair as I stare over the bench at his cognac Ferragamo Oxfords beneath me. He fists my hair so tightly that the pain radiating across my scalp causes me to momentarily forget about the current state of my ass and thighs.

Using his grip, he demandingly pulls my attention up to him. There is no denying the disappointment in his dark-chestnut eyes when I meet his gaze. Bending toward my face, he lowers his voice and gruffs, "Are you fucking crying?"

The butterfly gag in my mouth leaves me incapable of responding, but my silence only further agitates him. He turns his fist, and my eyes blow wide as he pulls my hair so hard I swear it's tearing from my scalp.

"I thought you were going to be a good girl for me tonight." His gravelly whisper is as dark and cold as his stare. His ire grows with every word that passes over his lips. "Instead, you are making me look bad before all these people. Letting them think I have a poorly trained submissive who can't even handle a fucking paddling."

He stoops down to my level, and his nostrils flare as he sneers, "You're making me look like a weak fucking Dom. Is that what you wanted?"

His hold on me is so tight that I can barely move when I try to shake my head to refute his question.

"No?" Isaac mocks, releasing his excruciatingly tight hold of my hair. He glances to the crowd beyond the window and a fake smile pulls at the corners of his mouth as he returns his attention to me. His fingers tenderly wiping the tears from my cheeks are a stark contrast to his devilish dark tone. "And how are you going to fix this?"

Knowing the answer he's going to give me, I gulp, and it's like I'm choking on the gag in my mouth.

"We need to show them how well I've trained you, don't we?" he rhetorically asks, and my stomach sinks.

I can't.

Not that it matters, because it never does. He'll prove to me I *can*. If I protest, he'll prove it some more. "Now nod your fucking head that you agree."

Fighting back more tears and knowing I'm putting my life in his hands, I nod to please him. *Anything to please him.* This gag is suffocating and every tear I cry only causes my nose to become more congested. The only relief I can provide myself is going to slowly kill me when he inflicts my punishment for making him look poorly before the other members of the club.

He lifts the bulb to the gag in my mouth and squeezes slowly, fully inflating it and further constricting my breathing. He gives another partial squeeze, the gag feeling like it might explode in my mouth, as he whispers darkly, "Be a good little bitch and fucking take it. Show them how well I've fucking trained you."

From the corner of my eye, I watch Isaac lift the cat o' nine tails from the edge of the bed to my right. He wastes no time swinging it, and the sharp sting slices through my already tender skin. Tears stream down my cheeks as the subsequent strikes feel like they're clawing through my flesh.

My fat, silent sobs slowly fill my nose with mucus. Hopelessly, I struggle to breathe, and my heart pounds ungodly hard against the bench. Unable to draw in air around the gag or through my snot-filled nose, I futilely try to get Isaac's attention. I pull frantically at my restraints as my lungs burn, spasming as they try desperately to draw in the oxygen I can't.

Oh, God! Please... Someone help me.

The crowd on the other side of the window has thinned drastically, and my wide, terror-filled eyes don't garner anyone's attention. Blackness creeps at the edges of my vision as I find a pair of kind, concerned eyes beyond the pane of glass. He's the last thing I see before everything goes black.

CHAPTER TWO
LIAM

"You're a fucking asshole, Liam," Ella crossly proclaims, without making eye contact with me. With her back turned away from me, she pulls handfuls of clothes from the dresser and haphazardly tosses them into the suitcase strewn open on the bed. She drops her current armful to the quickly growing pile as her angry, tear-filled eyes meet mine, and she huffs, "Really?"

"Really, *what*, El?" I shrug, knowing exactly where this argument is going. The same place it always does. Only this time, it's worse.

"You aren't going to say anything!" she exclaims, throwing her arms into the air.

Standing from leaning against the door frame, I cross the room to close the distance between us. I cup her face and gaze down into her hazy green eyes—*knowing damn well what she wants to hear*—I exhale, "What do you want me to say?"

Ella is practically perfect—*everything I didn't know I wanted*—a well-educated, dominant queen in her work life who is an impeccable submissive. Her long and lean, athletically toned body is built for the pain she loves to receive from me. The gorgeous woman staring into my eyes has only one flaw. She wants the one thing in this world I can't give her.

The one thing I'd never give any *woman.*

"I've told you, El." I slide my bloodied hands from her cheeks, inadvertently leaving them stained with a ruddy hue. "They're my family. I know this life scares you—"

"Scares me?" she snaps. "Fucking look at yourself."

I don't need to glance into the mirror to see what she's demanding. My shirt is torn and stained crimson. The blood covering my hands is my own, from clutching to the—now-sutured—knife wound above my right hip.

"I love you, Liam. *I* want to be your family," Ella sobs as she wipes the tears running down her blood-smeared cheeks. Her eyes run over my tattered appearance, and she sniffles. "But I can't do it like this."

"El, baby, I didn't say it would be easy," I try to console her, "but look at Dec and Sarah. They're married. They're having a baby. The two of them are so fucking happy."

Ella shoves herself from me, and she mutters, "You all are really that oblivious."

"Oblivious to what?"

"Sarah is fucking terrified!" she shouts. "She married Declan because she loves him, but don't for a second think that she doesn't worry each and every time he walks out of their apartment. She lives with the very real fear that he won't come home and that she's going to wind up raising that baby all alone."

"She would *never* be alone," I gruffly correct her. "None of us would let that happen. While we could never replace Declan, all of us would step up to be a father."

Closing the lid on her suitcase, tears continue to stream down Ella's face as she zips it shut. "That's just it, Li—"

"What?" I ask for clarification as she slides the heavy suitcase off the bed. It hits the hardwood floor with a thud. The sound reverberates around the silent room, followed by the clicks of the telescoping handle and the heart-wrenching sound of the wheels dragging along the wood.

"I want to marry you, Liam," Ella says between sobs. Stopping before me, she stares up at me with teary, bloodshot eyes as she releases the suitcase. She drops her gaze to her hand and swallows hard as she grasps the diamond adorning her ring finger. While slowly pulling it from her digit, she repeats herself, "I want to marry *you*, Liam. But I don't want to wind up with your brothers as my consolation prize when you don't come home one night."

Gripping my hand, she places her engagement ring in the center of my palm and closes my fist around it. She lifts it to her face and places a soft kiss on the back of my hand, whispering, "I love you, Liam."

"Fuck, El.," I plead as she drops my hand. "I love you."

Ella grabs her suitcase and drags it to the door before pausing on the threshold. Without turning back to face me, she mutters, "I know you do, Li. But sometimes... Love isn't enough."

Unable to move from where I stand for fear she'll shove me away, I beg, "Don't do this. Please, El."

Rooted in place, Ella's hand tightly grips the suitcase. She lets out a deep breath as she lifts her head and rolls her shoulders back, leaving her standing tall in the doorway. After clearing her throat, her tone is devoid of emotion when she requests, "Don't contact me. Just let me go."

As much as I want to chase after the heels clicking through my apartment, I do as she asks.

Clutching the ring, it tears into my palm. Droplets of fresh blood trickle from my grasp and run down my arm, but I can't feel the pain. My heavy footsteps carry me across the room. I reach the doorway to the hall just in time to hear the front door latching.

"El…" I call, clinging to the hope that she wasn't able to find the will to actually walk from this apartment—*and from my life*—only to be quickly met with devastating silence.

"Fuck!" I roar, driving my bloodied fist through the wall.

Walking back into the bedroom, I pull open the drawer to the valet sitting atop my dresser and drop the now sticky, crimson ring into it. Pushing it shut, I exhale the breath I've been holding.

Never again.

CHAPTER THREE
SASHA

ABOUT ONE YEAR AGO

"Please…" I beg through sobs.

Shawn tightens his agonizing hold on the back of my neck in response, and I wince as my shoulders rise to ease the pressure. His fingertips dimple my skin as he pulls me back to meet his heated gaze. Staring down at me, he snarls, "If I had known you were this incapable of following instructions, I never would've taken your fat ass off Trevor's hands. They are simple rules, Sasha."

Denying him is against his rules—*I know that*—but I'm so sore from last night that I can't fathom being able to tolerate him touching me again.

One morning. One measly morning in seven months that he didn't get to push inside me. *That's all I wanted.*

"What happens to disobedient little whores?" he growls.

"I'm sorry." I feign an apology, hoping that he's lenient.

"Stupid bitch. I didn't ask if you were fucking sorry." Using his grip on my neck, Shawn roughly leads me through the house and into the kitchen. My eyes dart around the stark white surroundings, seeking his form of punishment, as he opens multiple cabinets. A dark chuckle rises from his lungs as he pulls a silver cylinder from the top shelf.

"I only take my apologies one way," he snarks as a devilish smirk pulls at the corners of his lips. He releases his grip to open the container and I rub the tender skin that is probably already bruising. The metal lid clangs when he tosses it to the granite countertop, and he pours out the contents of the container. Tiny grains of rice rain over my bare feet and bounce when they hit the cold tile floor. His gaze falls to the floor, and he demands, "Kneel."

This can't possibly be worse than the paddling I took a few nights ago when I didn't dress to his exacting standards for dinner.

I hesitantly place my knee into the thin layer of uncooked rice, grimacing as I shift my weight to drop my other knee.

This is worse than the paddle. Far worse!

The thin grains puncture my skin like tiny shards of glass beneath me. Seconds tick by like hours as I try to ignore the stabbing pain in my knees and shins.

"You will learn to obey me," Shawn whispers, his soft tone making his threat much more terrifying. Cupping my chin, he holds it firmly as he squats before me. His face inches from mine, he watches as my pained tears roll down my cheeks. "You can tell me now."

"I... I'm... sorry, Sir," I repeat my previous unwelcome apology between sobs.

"Don't cry. I love you. I'll do whatever it takes to teach you how to behave for me." Shawn wipes his thumb across my cheek and rubs the salty collection of tears over my lower lip as he asks, "And what are you sorry for?"

"Denying... you... Sir."

Pressing his salty thumb into my mouth, he rubs it over my tongue as he asks, "And are you allowed to deny me the pleasure I get from being inside you?"

I suck on his thumb as he pulls it from my mouth. He sloppily rubs my saliva over my lips as I answer, "No."

"Learning already," he praises as a slight smile spreads across his face. Shawn rises to his feet and asks, "Are you going to give me what I wanted?"

"Yes, Sir," I quickly answer, painfully shifting my weight to one leg. I begin to push myself from the floor as his fingers work to hastily undo his belt.

"What do you think you're doing?" Shawn gruffs, quickly gripping my shoulder and firmly pressing me back into the rice. My face contorts as the shards jam back into my skin. I listen to him undoing the teeth of his zipper as he crunches through the rice to close the distance between us. "You can get up when you prove you've learned your lesson."

With my jaw clenched in agony, I open my eyes and find his pants splayed. The dirty blond tuft of his hair rests between the parted zipper, and he is rapidly growing hard in the tight confines of his boxer briefs.

"I'm not a monster, Sasha. I will not force you to swallow my cock." He pushes the hair from my tear-stained cheeks and tucks it behind my ear. For as cruel as he can be, in this aspect at least, he treats me better than Trevor—or his friends—ever did. Staring up at him, my throat bobs as I swallow hard, and he shares, "You're going to do it willingly because you want to show me what a good little submissive you are. Because you want to prove you're as devoted to serving me as I am to helping you be better."

Lifting my hands from my trembling thighs, I grip the waistband of his pants. I pull them down his thighs, and his hard length springs free. Wrapping my hand around the base of his shaft, I run my tongue along the ridge of the head before sucking him into my mouth. He groans in pleasure as I quickly slide my lips over his length, repeatedly filling my throat with all of him. Hollowing my cheeks and desperately needing him to come, I suck his cock with such vigor that spittle runs down my chin and over his balls.

"You really *are* fucking sorry," he grits through his heavy, labored breaths as he fights his need to come. He fists the edge of the counter for balance as he spills his sour seed onto my tongue. I choke it down, hoping to remove the vile taste from my mouth. "That's it. Swallow every drop of your breakfast."

Shawn tucks his spent cock back into his pants and gestures for me to get up from the kneeling position. Rising from the floor is nearly as excruciating as suffering through the punishment. Grains of rice fall from deep dimples they've made in my skin, and the hollowed pockets of skin throb.

"When I get home from the office and want to fuck **my** pussy or **my** ass, what are you going to say?"

"Yes, Sir," I hastily answer with a quick nod.

"And if I bring home a friend to see what a good girl you are?"

Sucking in a sputtered breath, I try to hold back my tears when I reply, "Yes, Sir."

A proud smile beams across his face, yet his eyes remain devoid of emotion. "And why is that?"

"Because it's my job to please you, Sir."

"That's better. You might turn out to be a decent submissive yet," he imparts as he walks from the kitchen. Without breaking his stride, he calls over his shoulder, "Clean yourself up nice for me so I can show you off. Isaac and I will be here about seven."

CHAPTER FOUR

LIAM

"Sir," Jorge announces as he slides a freshly poured glass of Jameson before me. "This is from the blonde in the red dress."

My eyes drag down the bar, and for a brief, surprising second, I hope to magically find Ella sitting at the other end.

It isn't her.

Where the fuck did that come from?

It's been over five years since I've seen or heard from her. She packed up her entire life and disappeared without a trace within days of walking from my apartment; she knew before I did that I wouldn't be able to let her walk away. If I didn't have tangible proof she was real, I would probably wonder if I had actually dreamed her into existence.

"Jorge," I huff. "For the love of Christ, if you aren't fucking kneeling for me, don't call me Si—"

"You know I would"—Jorge winks at me—"Sir." Before I have a chance to argue with his bratty ass, he returns to our paying patrons as Conor and Finn laugh.

I mutter under my breath, "Jesus fucking Chr…"

"I know you fucking suck at this"—Finn elbows me hard—"but this is the point where you walk your ass over there and talk to her."

The woman lifting her glass and smiling at me is beautiful. That much is undeniable. She'd likely be fun tonight. We might even have fun for a few months. But like Ella put it so eloquently—and I've been ruminating about this more than usual for the past few days because of the ache in my left shoulder from a fresh bullet wound—the women I date want to be with *me*, not worried they're going to wind up alone and being cared for by my brothers.

"Are you trying to take Declan's former seat as president of the Grumpy Old Men Blowing Loads of Dust Club?" Finn nudges me again with a chuckle.

After taking a hearty sip of the warm amber liquid, I place the glass back on the bar top before answering, "You do know that I'm not celibate, right?"

"Are you sure? You realize that you're turning down a definite opportunity to get your dick wet?" Finn raises a brow as he poses the rhetorical question. Making a checkmark with his hand in the air when I don't respond, he vehemently confirms, "Celibate."

Squeezing the glass in my hand, I fight the urge to deck him. Finn might be the most vocal about it, but all my brothers give me shit about my virtually non-existent love life. I got a pass for a while—*they all know how much I loved her*—but that seems to have expired. Apparently, if Declan can move on after mourning his deceased wife, I should be able to get over the woman who broke my heart.

It's my love life that's non-existent, not my sex life. By choice, I'm aromantic. *Definitely not fucking celibate.* I fuck plenty. I just ensure that there is virtually no chance that I'll become emotionally invested in them. The women I enjoy just happen to be either one-night stands or well-negotiated, short-term Master/slave relationships.

Attempting to change the subject, I gruff, "What the fuck are you doing here, anyway?"

"Seriously," Conor interjects. "You literally just married one of the hottest fucking women I've ever seen. Why the fuck are you sitting here with us assholes?"

"I happen to like the lot of you," Finn replies. "And Cat begged me to give her a few hours to study in peace without me trying to distract her."

"And you listened?" I over-exaggerate my surprise.

"I did." Finn laughs. "It was a trade-off. In exchange for her few hours alone, she's going to read to me when I get home."

Conor turns on his barstool, and his face contorts in confusion as he exclaims, "The trade is that your gorgeous-as-sin wife is going to read you a bedtime story?"

"Yup. Catlin has to read *Lady Chatterley's Lover* for her Lit course. So, she's been reading it to me." Finn downs the final sip of whiskey in the glass before him as he stands from his bar stool. His ever-cheeky smile spreads across his face, and he shares, "More correctly, Catlin tries to try to read it while she sits on my face."

"I really fucking hate him sometimes," I huff as Declan takes Finn's now-empty seat.

"Just sometimes?" Declan chimes. "I could beat the piss out of him at least twice a day."

Taking a sip of my whiskey, I turn to the woman at the end of the bar and am relieved to find that another man has garnered her attention. Hating the semi-accuracy of Finn's jokes, I slide my half-finished glass before Declan and mutter, "I'm going to head out."

"Please tell me you didn't blow off that gorgeous blonde to go home and pine over a ghost," Conor grouses.

"No," I scoff. I don't sit at home and mope over the woman I thought was going to be my wife. *Until tonight, it's been nearly a year since she has flittered through my thoughts.* "I've just had enough of your ugly mug for the night, and I'm sure Dec is only a drink away from talking about how he needs to knock up his wife again."

"Already tried this morning," Declan smirks, "and again before I came to the club."

"Jesus." I sigh with a laugh. "I was fucking kidding. You know it can just be a fun kink and that you don't *actually* have to make Quinn birth an entire rugby team."

Leaving Conor and Declan at the bar in the lounge, I walk from the club to head home. It's nearly 2 a.m., my shoulder is fucking killing me, and by the time I reach my bedroom, all I can think about is stripping out of this suit and climbing into bed. *To sleep.*

After tossing my suit jacket to the settee at the foot of the bed, I remove my cufflinks as I make my way across the room. I pull the second one free as I reach the dresser. When I pull open the drawer to the valet to put them away, my eyes are immediately drawn to the blood-crusted diamond ring tucked in the corner.

I should get rid of it. Sell it. Pawn it. Or simply flush it down the fucking toilet. Any sentimental attachments I had to it are long gone, like the love I once felt for Ella. These days, it merely serves as a reminder:

Never again.

CHAPTER FIVE
SASHA

"Your drink, Sir." I place Shawn's freshly poured vodka and tonic beside him. It's the fifth very heavy pour I've filled for him in a couple of hours, and he's already quite drunk. Placing the other two glasses before Isaac, I inform him, "And your two doubles of tequila on the rocks."

Isaac looks at the glasses and back at me as he wraps his fingers around one. His eyes not leaving mine, he slowly slides it across the table toward me. "That's for you, beautiful. I loved watching you suck him off, but I would prefer your mouth didn't taste like Shawn's cum when I stick my tongue in it."

Shawn has always enjoyed sharing me, but he has never shared me with any of his friends this frequently. In the beginning, Isaac visited from New York every couple of weeks, but lately, I see him at least twice a week. This trip was unexpected, and the first time that Isaac has stayed for more than a night. The two of them have passed me between them, at Isaac's behest, for the past three days.

Something happened between them—*something I'm not privy to*—but Shawn is clearly not in charge anymore. The man who used to fuck me every morning and night has barely touched me for the past three days. *And he only does when Isaac tells him to.*

Not enjoying a sloppy fuck, Shawn has kept me sober the entire time he's owned me. I glance at him as I lift the glass from the table, but he doesn't so much as blink when I press it to my lips. Parting them, I swallow a mouthful of the clear liquid. It burns as it slides down my throat. "Finish it." Isaac's hand envelops mine, and he tips the glass, forcing me to finish the remaining shot in the glass.

"She seems to listen for me," Isaac snarks as he roughly pulls me into his lap. His lips crash against mine, and he aggressively pushes his tongue into my mouth. He kisses me hard as his hands roam my body with the same forceful need. Retreating from our kiss, Isaac holds my lower lips firmly between his teeth. It's teasingly light. Playful. And very not like Isaac. I whimper into his mouth as nips at my lower lip. My mewl quickly grows into a pained cry when he slowly bites through the thin flesh until my mouth fills with the bitter taste of copper. He sucks at the painful bite, soothing my discomfort and drawing my blood into his mouth with a groan of delight.

There's the Isaac I know.

"It's a shame you're all the way up here in Connecticut." Isaac pulls my camisole over my head and haphazardly tosses it in Shawn's direction. He leaves a trail of painful bite marks on my shoulder and down to my bare breasts as he shares, "I'd prefer to have you locked up in my penthouse in Manhattan, where I could enjoy you like this whenever I wanted."

He grabs his glass of tequila from the table and takes both shots into his mouth before pulling me back into him. Squeezing my jaw, the tequila burns over the fresh wound in my lip as he spits the contents of his mouth into mine. He holds my face up, forcing me to swallow back the mouthful of tequila. A wicked smile spreads across his face and he praises, "That's a good girl."

Fuck, I love that! Shawn never tells me what a good girl I am for him. *Actually, he never praises me.* He tells me how to be good for him and then lets me know how I'm not doing well enough.

Isaac slides me from his lap to my suddenly unsteady feet. After not having had a drop of alcohol in almost a year, the shots he had me drink a few minutes ago hit me much harder and faster than I expected them to. I hold the table beside me for balance as he undoes the button to my shorts and pushes them down my legs with my panties. After spinning me around, he quickly bends me over the table. I hit it with such force it rattles the glasses on it. Isaac presses himself against my entrance and shoves the entirety of him into my unprepared pussy, causing me to cry out as he painfully enters me.

"That's it. Let Shawn know how much you prefer *my* cock," he croons, thrusting into me. Turning his attention to Shawn, he condescends through the repeated drive of his hips, "I never hear her cry for you like this."

His fingers slip into my hair and he tightens a fist, yanking my gaze up to Shawn. His chest is heaving, and his nostrils flare slightly, watching Isaac fuck me, but he says nothing.

"Fucking pussy," Isaac spits at Shawn as his savage thrusts repeatedly drive my hips into the rough edge of the table. "No wonder she'd rather be with me."

Wait?

Tightening his hold on my hair with his left hand, Isaac's right firmly connects with my ass. It hits with such force that I bite through my already tattered and bloody lip. When I open my mouth to speak, the only sound that passes my lips is a yelp as his hand strikes me again. "Tell him, beautiful," Isaac demands, "Tell him you want to be mine."

What?

Intoxicated and confused, I try to understand what the fuck is happening right now. Isaac's hips grind against the heated flesh of my backside as he bends over me and whispers in my ear, "If he really wanted you, he never would've shared you with me. I don't let other men fuck my property."

Isaac pulls from me, rolls me onto my back and slams into me again. He buries himself to the hilt before lifting me to meet him. Using my hair to force me to hold his gaze, he gruffs, "No one wants you like I do."

"You want me?" I breathlessly try to clear my confusion through his thrusts. *No one ever wants me.*

Nodding his answer, Isaac drives me to the brink. His teeth sink into my neck, and the pain pushes me over the edge, causing me to cry out my release. The room spins, and my vision goes blurry, leaving me unsure if it's the alcohol or my euphoric high. With his fingers laced tightly around my throat, Isaac snarls, "Now, tell Shawn who this tight, quivering pussy belongs to."

Is this what it's like to be truly wanted?

"You," I slur when he loosens his hold on my neck to allow my answer.

In my next moment of brief clarity, I find myself on my stomach and unsure of where I am. *When did we move to the bedroom?* Isaac continues to slam his hips against the searing pain that is my ass and thighs, driving me into the softness of a mattress with every brutal thrust. Blackness creeps in and out of my vision, and I repeatedly wake to find myself in different positions as Isaac enjoys all of me.

With my legs on his shoulders, Isaac slides into me with long, deep strokes. He quickens his pace and empties himself into me before collapsing against my chest, whispering, "Now that you're mine, I can and will enjoy you like that every night, beautiful."

Yours? He hasn't just been coming to fuck me. Unlike Shawn, Isaac really wants me.

He places a rough, dry kiss against my lips and slides from me before rolling to the other side of the bed. As he pulls the covers over himself, he instructs, "You can sleep here, but you need to go clean yourself up. I don't want to wake up with my cum all over me."

CHAPTER SIX

LIAM

"You can't be serious," Finn chimes from the back seat of the Suburban. "We aren't really going to sit down with the Russian assholes?"

We've been fighting the Bratva since the night Finn beat the shit out of some accountant nobody at Kiska nearly three years ago. It crests and ebbs like tides in the ocean, but it's been a constant threat to us all. Especially to the ones we all hold dear—Quinn, Fiona, Layla, Catlin, little Rory, and Kira—the ones least able to protect themselves. We all knew that killing the Pakhan at Our Lady of Grace wouldn't be the end of the war.

That end was just a new beginning.

It was only a matter of time before the Bratva decided among themselves who would take the Pakhan's place.

Ivan Levedeva. A *brigadier* who has been serving in the Bratva since he was only a *lad*. Rumor has it he made his first kill at the age of twelve. He was functioning as a *kryshas* by the time he was sixteen and earned his thieves' stars before hitting twenty. The only reason he wasn't already Pakhan is probably the fact that he spent the past five years in Polar Wolf.

"Seriously? Hello?" Finn chirps when his initial statement doesn't warrant a response from any of us. "You're going to make me sit in the back *and* ignore me?"

"For fuck's sake, Finn," Declan huffs from the seat beside me. "We're literally heading to Tristan's to talk it out. And you sit in the back because that's the safest place for children."

"Quinn definitely didn't think I was childish when Cat and I visited her this afternoon." Finn's snark carries a mischievous smirk in it.

"That's it!" Declan unfastens his seatbelt and clambers into the backseat with the agility of a man half his age, landing a hard punch on Finn's face. Conor slips his arms under Declan's and pulls him from Finnigan before he has a chance to land another fist, and Finn groans, "Fuck, Dec. It was a fucking joke."

"Everything is a fucking joke with you," Declan growls, struggling against Conor's firm hold. "This whole fucking mess started because you couldn't keep your dick in your pants."

"You think I don't know that?" Finn huffs.

"Fuck!" I pull to a stop at the curb outside Tristan's building. "Maybe instead of meeting Tris, we can take the two of you to group therapy. You can talk this shit out."

"*Póg mo thóin*," Declan and Finn spit, nearly in unison.

"So we're better?" I spin in my seat and get my first glimpse at Finn's bloodied face. "Or do Conor and I need to leave the two of you in the car to beat the piss out of each other again?"

"Each other?" Declan scoffs as he pushes open the door and climbs over Finn to exit the SUV. "I'm not the one with blood dripping down my face." The three of us follow behind into Tristan's building, past security, and straight to the waiting cab of the elevator.

Wiping his face, Finn spits a mouthful of blood onto the white-tiled floor of the elevator as it opens at Tristan's apartment. "Jesus, Finn!" Layla exclaims, reaching out to tenderly touch his bloody lower lip as we all step from the cab. "Did you piss off Catlin? Or make an untimely joke about fucking Quinn again?"

"Untimely joke," he answers, allowing her to inspect his bloodied face. "I didn't even get the chance to drop the Viagra one I've been holding on to for a week."

"I'll get you some ice. But I'll be honest, Finn, I don't know how he hasn't killed you yet." She gives him a gentle pat on the chest.

"You and the rest of us," I quip.

By the time Layla returns with a bag of ice for Finn's lip, the five of us have situated ourselves around the fire pit on the penthouse terrace. Tristan eyes a still-searing Declan and Finn nursing his lip before informing of us about his call with Ivan and a proposed truce between us.

"I don't trust it," Declan gives his opinion. "Blood and violence have been Ivan's life for over two decades, and now he suddenly wants peace."

"I'm with Dec," Conor agrees.

"I can't take back the stupid shit I did," Finn blurts before addressing Declan's accusation in the SUV and delving into shit that none of us ever talk about. While he's still the sarcastic, playful shit we have all grown to love, something about Catlin has changed him for the better. Forced him to grow up. He's still unhinged and impulsive as fuck, but he now owns how that affects us all. "But don't for a second think that I don't blame myself for what happened to Quinn. What could've happened to Layla or my peanut. Or how they almost took Cat from me."

"So, your vote?" Tristan presses.

"I'd do anything to ensure Cat, Layla, Quinn, and those kids are safe," he promises, and for a moment, even Declan appears to soften a little toward him. "And if that means we sit down with the Pakhan... so be it."

"I can't believe I'm saying this." I shake my head and say something I never thought would leave my mouth. "I agree with Finn. This is about doing whatever it takes to keep those you—no, *we*—all love safe. And if that means meeting our enemy, then we pull up a chair at that table."

"Agree," Tristan nods.

"Fine," Declan huffs. "But I swear to Christ, if I get shot again, I'm blaming Finn."

"Same," Conor chimes.

"What the fuck?" Finn mutters through the bag of ice pressed to his now-swollen lip. "Since when are you on his side?"

A coy smile tugs at Conor's lips as he quips, "I'm still salty about being denied the opportunity to see Cat's cotton panties."

"I thought we were clear about that," Finn barks, his hands gesturing at Conor. "No thinking about my wife's panties."

"Apparently, none of you listen," I gruff, rising from my seat. "Because I'm pretty sure that fat lip is a reminder that you aren't supposed to be cracking jokes about fucking Quinn."

CHAPTER SEVEN
SASHA

"And who do you belong to?" Isaac presses as he holds me on his lap, his hard length rubbing against me.

My eyes dart over the desk at the two men across from us. They are both pretending to be invested in their private conversation, but they are watching us with curious intent. I swallow hard before answering, "You, Sir."

"Show me," he whispers in my ear.

"Sir?" I whisper-blurt, uncertain of what he's asking of me.

Isaac's fingers pull at the hemline of the white bodycon dress he insisted I wear tonight, not stopping until it bunches at the top of my thighs, barely covering my pantyless pussy. The desk between us and the two men is currently the only thing keeping them from an unfettered view of me. Their eyes keep darting in our direction, and I'm certain they both know exactly what is happening.

His lips and teeth graze along the back of my shoulder as he reaches between us to undo his pants. "You're going to be a good girl and sit nice and still on my cock while I have this meeting," he quietly instructs before shifting his hips. Lifting me slightly, he shoves himself into me at a painfully awkward angle, and I fight the urge to cry out. He leans us both toward the desk, sinking deeper into me as he gravelly whispers, "Show me how well you can listen, and I'll make you mine. Forever."

Reaching to the desk drawer beside us, he pulls out a black folder and a matching velvet gift box.

"Sir?" I whisper, tears of joy prickle my eyes as he opens his folder for the meeting. I have done everything Issac has asked of me for the two months since he moved me to his apartment in New York. He's a demanding Dom, and at times, it feels as though he's impossible to please. He has repeatedly told me he wanted me more than Shawn, how much he loves me, and now he's going to prove it. *He wants to ensure I'm his forever.* The box before me is far too big to be a ring, but it's the perfect size for a collar.

"Shhh," he hushes me as one of the two gentlemen across from us begins to talk about margins, stock options, and other topics I have very little understanding of.

The meeting between the three men is boring. Even Isaac is losing interest. He's spent more of this meeting paying attention to the velvet gift box twirling between his fingers than either of his colleagues. How he has managed to stay hard through the last hour of drab mergers and acquisitions talk is absolutely baffling.

"Throw in your ties, gentlemen, and we have a deal." Isaac smiles and stretches his hand across the table.

"Our ties?" The blond man—*Dwight, I think*—looks at Isaac and back to the associate beside him.

"Sasha really likes them. Don't you, beautiful?"

"Yes, Sir. I like them both very much."

Confusion flits across both their faces, and the men across from us loosen the knots of their ties. One at a time, they toss them to the center of the leather pad covering the desk and in turn shake Isaac's firm hand. Grabbing the ties and pulling them toward us, Issac stares up at two men as he undoes one of the knotted ties. "We're done here. I assume you can see yourselves out so I can properly celebrate my victory."

"Oh," the middle-aged man startles upon realizing what Isaac is inferring. He nudges the blond, and the two of them quickly leave us alone in Isaac's office.

Slipping the silk tie under my left knee, Isaac uses the fabric to pull my leg over his thigh. He loops it around the armrest and demands my hand. I provide it willingly, and he affixes the loose end around my wrist. When he cinches it tight, my arm and leg are bound firmly to the chair. He repeats the process on my right leg with the other tie, leaving my thighs spread wide as I straddle his lap.

"Are you sure you want to be mine?" Isaac asks, running his fingers along the length of my inner thighs. "I demand excellence. Perfection. And no matter how much I love you, I will not be lenient when I don't receive it."

"Understood, Sir."

"Do you agree to follow your Sir without hesitation?"

"Yes, Sir."

"And to obey without question?"

"Yes, Sir."

"After I mark you tonight, you'll always be mine."

"Mark me?" I mumble the words racing through my thoughts so softly that Isaac doesn't hear them. My heart pounds as Isaac lays the box he's been fidgeting with flat on the desk. He takes his time teasingly lifting the lid, slowly revealing the red velvet interior. Opening it further, I see the "gift" inside, and my stomach drops.

Definitely not a ring.

Or a collar.

Isaac lifts the all-black knife from the box and holds it before my face as I repeat myself. Only this time, the words quiver with the trembling of my lower lip. "Mark me?"

"Yes, beautiful. I'm going to mark you." He presses the point of the blade against my knee, dragging it up my inner thigh just light enough that it scratches but doesn't break the skin. Running it over the bare mound of my pussy, his voice is deep and gravelly when he shares, "If it wouldn't take so long to heal, I'd carve my name into the plump lips of your cunt so you could never deny who it belongs to."

I tense at his words as my chest heaves with a mixture of nervous excitement and fear. Realizing the restraints securing me firmly in place aren't for fun, I tug violently at the silk.

"Relax," Isaac whispers, dragging the blade back to the fleshy part of my inner thigh. "I'm about to give you exactly what you want. When I'm done, you'll always be mine."

Before I can mutter a single word of my rebuttal, Isaac swipes the blade. My blood trickles from the wound and down my inner thigh for a second before my brain registers the pain. By the time I let out my first cry, Isaac is slicing through my skin again. His cock throbs and grows more rigid inside me with every pained scream that rattles from my lungs as he continues to carve through my flesh. Tears stream down my cheeks, and I silently sob as he carves the final letter, the blade brushing against my pussy as he finishes.

"Good girl," he praises, dropping the knife from his bloodied hand and spreading me wider to admire his handiwork. His hands slide over my dress, smearing stains of scarlet over it as he undulates his hips to slide his rigid cock in and out of me. Crimson rushes down my leg, and he smears it over my thighs, biting my shoulders with enough force to draw blood from them, too.

Quickly untying the knots, Isaac lifts me into him. I wrap my arms around his neck, I try to press my lips to his. He denies me his mouth and drops my back onto the desk with a thud that knocks the breath from my lungs. As I struggle to catch my breath, he splays my legs and plows into me. He holds my legs wide and smears the sticky ruby liquid along every inch of my thigh. Tears well in my eyes as he drives into me with a new level of brutality, every thrust more painful than the last. Staring down at me with dark, evil eyes, he grunts between the clap of his hips against my ass and thighs, "Who... do... you... belong... to?"

Isaac lifts my leg and wraps his hands around it to hold me in place as he slams into me. I know he asked me a question, but it didn't register in my agonized brain. Every bit of my focus is on the blood oozing from the meticulous marks Isaac left on me.

ISAAC

Branded as his, forever.

Pain explodes through my eyes when his bloodied palm lands on my cheek, snapping my attention back to him. I meet his dark gaze, and he snarls, "Who do you fucking belong to?"

His fingers flex painfully hard, digging his short fingernails into my skin, and he buries himself inside me with a groan. He spills his release inside me, and tears trickle down my face as I whisper, "You, Sir."

Forever.

CHAPTER EIGHT
LIAM

Declan, Tristan, Conor, Rory, and—surprisingly—Finn have been silent during our drive from Declan's place in New Rochelle. Our meeting with the new Pakhan has been a month in the making, and even though we've taken extreme precautions for our safety, I'm pretty sure all of us are on edge.

Merging into traffic, I drive down West 52nd Street and turn into the valet parking garage. The six of us take a moment to stow our guns and knives beneath each of our seats before climbing from the Tahoe. The valet takes my keys in exchange for a retrieval ticket, and we make the short walk down the bustling block to the Museum of Modern Art.

Approaching the line full of families and high-school-aged kids on field trips, Declan asks, "Anyone else feel a little out of place?"

This was an odd-as-fuck place to choose for this meeting.

"It checks all the boxes." Finn shrugs. "Public and populated."

"And when this goes south and they break the agreement not to bring guns, they'll only have killed all of us, a few families, and half of P.S. 35," Conor jests, causing the woman in front of him to spin around with a horrified look on her face.

"He's kidding." I laugh with a playful nod, trying to play off his honest concern. "He has a terrible sense of humor." When she finally turns back around, I toss up my hands and mouth, *"What the fuck?"*

An awkward smile and furrowed brow paint Conor's face, and he silently says, *"Sorry."*

Why worry about the Bratva when we can just get taken out by security for making mass shooting threats?

As we make our way inside, we each scan the e-ticket from our phones and pass through the metal security detector. We walk through the lobby of the first floor, toward the Rockefeller Sculpture Garden. Out of earshot of the security guards, Finn snarks at Declan, "Still think it's a stupid location?" Declan rolls his eyes in response, which only seems to push Finn to agitate him further. "C'mon. You can say it: This was a good idea, Finn."

"How did *you,* of all people, know about this place anyway?" I ask.

"Cat likes the paintings," Finn answers with a shrug, a mischievous smile tugging at the corner of his mouth. "And I enjoy getting my wife off in public."

And there it is...

"For fuck's sake," Declan exhales as we walk outside into the garden. "Here? You fucked Catlin here?"

"No. I made her come *here*." Pointing toward the back corner occupied by a large wave-shaped sculpture, he smirks. "Right over there, actually. But now that you mention it."

It's like Finn knows *exactly* what to say to get under Declan's skin. *Every single time.* Sucking in a deep breath, Declan lets out a heavy sigh and grumbles, "Someone shut him up. Please."

I check my watch for the time. 10:55 a.m.

Five heavily tattooed suit-clad men step into the garden and begin walking toward us, with a tall, dark-haired man—comparable in age to us—leading the way. *Ivan.* Even knowing they have all walked through the same metal detector we did, we all stiffen and become more vigilant of our surroundings.

"I thought there were five Evans brothers," Ivan observes with a slight Russian accent.

"He's adopted." Tristan glances at Rory, who stands out from the rest of us with his red hair. It's an honest answer. He might not be blood, but he's spilled enough of his own for this family to make him as much my brother as any of the other men standing beside me.

"I'll keep this short," Ivan offers. "We have two choices. We can keep shedding blood, which I will highly enjoy. Or... I can take your gift of eliminating Mikhail and putting me in his place as a gift. One that I repay with a truce."

"A truce?" Declan repeats. "And what does that look like?"

"The Big Apple is a huge fucking city. You stay out of our business and we'll stay out of yours."

The six of us look at each other, silently coming to an agreed-upon decision. Tristan outstretches his hand to Ivan as he says, "My brothers and I can agree to that."

This seems too fucking easy.

Ivan slaps his hand into Tristan's and shakes it firmly. "But if you fuck me"—Ivan's gaze slowly passes between Declan and Finn—"I will not fail as Mikhail did."

Finn stays quiet and stoic beside me—exercising self-restraint or biting the fuck out of his tongue—but I can practically feel the rage radiating off Declan as he exhales a quiet, angered breath.

Not releasing Ivan's hand, Tristan rebuts, "Cross us and we will send you to visit Mikhail."

A hearty, dark laugh rises from Ivan's chest. "Then we have an agreement."

A month to put together a three-minute meeting. One that I hope will eliminate the threats that those we love have had to suffer through since this war started.

Ivan and his men walk toward the gated exit for West 54th Street, and we head through the lobby to West 53rd Street. We make the quick—and silent—walk back to the parking garage. The valet delivers my Tahoe, and we all climb inside. As the final door clicks shut, Declan snarls, "If he ever fucking threatens my wife and children or Catlin again, I'll fucking kill him where he stands."

CHAPTER NINE
SASHA

"What the fuck are you wearing?" Isaac snarls when he walks through the front door. His eyes continue to roam over my unusually disheveled appearance as he waits for my answer.

Having spent the day in bed, I managed to pull myself from beneath the covers to greet him at the door as he requires of me. This cold hit me out of nowhere, and that was all I could muster. I didn't have the energy to shower or change into something he would deem appropriate. My congestion causes me to sound nasally and unintentionally sarcastic when I answer matter-of-factly, "Sweats."

"Do you think I'm fucking stupid?" Isaac spits, the soles of his shoes slapping against the hardwood floor as he angrily closes the distance between us. "I know they're fucking sweatpants. Why the fuck are you wearing them?"

"I... I'm... sorry," I stammer, stepping backward and trying to hold his angered gaze. *A look I have come to know all too well.* "I'm just really not feeling well."

Looming over me, his nostrils flare when he asks, "Do you know what today is?"

I do.

How could I not?

Finally being granted an invitation to the infamous Club Triskelion is the only thing Isaac has talked about for the past week. His giddiness only grew when he learned a couple of days ago that he had also secured an exhibition space for tonight. A room for him to showcase to the world everything he has been training me for during the past six months.

"I'm sorry, Sir." My voice trembles as I delve deep for courage, knowing I'm going to upset him. "I really don't feel up tonight."

A chuckle rattles from his chest, and the darkness of it causes goosebumps to prickle down my spine. He fists the front of my sweatshirt and yanks me toward him. I crash against his firm body as he shoves his other hand down the front of my pants. Brushing over my pussy to where he carved his name into my thigh, he rubs his hand over the raised flesh. He traces his fingers over the letters as he asks, "What does this mean?"

"That I'm yours," I sniffle as my nose runs.

"Maybe I've been too lenient," he fists my meaty upper thigh, causing me to hiss, "because it appears you've forgotten that being mine comes with rules."

Vigorously shaking my head, I vehemently state, "I'm not disobeying you, Sir. I just thought—"

"That's my job," he interrupts me. "I decide these things for you. And what did I decide?"

"That we're going to the club." I force a smile through the pain of his tight hold on me. My breathing is labored as I endure his squeeze, and I struggle to speak. "So you can show everyone how well you've trained me."

"Good girl," he purrs, releasing his hand. His fingers slide up my leg and dust over the lips of my bare pussy. He massages my mound as he continues, "Are you simply telling me what I want to hear?"

"No, Sir." I gasp when his fingers press between my lips and dust over my clit. I fist the front of his shirt as he rubs over the sensitive nub, struggling to maintain my balance as he tenderly touches me for the first time in weeks. "I want to show everyone how good I can be for you."

Isaac grips my throat and tips my face up toward his. His lips press against mine, and he swallows my whimpers as he slips two fingers deep inside me. With his tongue sweeping through my mouth, his fingers work deliberately to bring me to the edge. Riding his hand, his lips dust against mine as he whispers, "Not good, beautiful. Fucking perfect. You're going to be fucking perfect for me like I know you can."

While I know his rough, brutal hands are teaching me to be better for him, I'd do anything for *this* Isaac. The Isaac who adores me. When I please him, he can be so soft and loving. Hovering at the edge of my release, I pant, "Perfect. I'll be perfect for you."

"Promise?" he asks tenderly as I unfurl. Held in the strong arm of his embrace, my toes curl against the cool, hardwood floor as bliss shoots through me.

"Yes." My answer sounds like a plea for him to continue. A smirk pulls at his lips, loving the power he holds over me. "I'll do everything you demand of me."

Plunging his fingers deep, he curls them vigorously and quickly works me right to back the brink. "Then you can start right now," he demands, stilling his fingers and pulling them from me. "Remove those fucking clothes."

I hastily pull the hoodie over my head and toss it onto the floor as Isaac disappears down the hall. Pushing the bagging sweatpants down, I kick them from my feet. I'm standing naked and needy in the living room when Isaac returns, concealing something behind his back. Stepping back toward me, he places his hand on my shoulder. He gives a gentle squeeze and commands, "Get on your fucking knees."

Glancing at the hardwood floor, I swallow hard and drop to my knees—*my most hated position*—for him. He stands over me and tenderly rubs his fingers along my jaw. "I want to make sure you feel good before we leave," Isaac devilishly smirks as he pulls the toys from behind his back, revealing a large dildo and a wand. Kneeling behind me, he spits a generous amount of saliva on the dildo's head. He presses the entirety of it into my pussy, and I wince at the sudden stretch. After teasingly pulling it from me, he affixes the suction cup to the floor before cycling through the speeds on the wand. Settling on the second-highest one, he spreads the lips of my pussy and presses it firmly against my clit.

"I demand ten," he gravelly whispers his command in my ear, rubbing the wand vigorously over my clit as his free hand wraps around my throat and pulls me into him. "My perfect girl will ride that fat rubber cock and take them all without a fucking sound."

Every muscle in my body trembles, and my knees grind so painfully into the hardwood floor I swear there are grains of rice beneath them. Yet, I struggle silently through the first seven orgasms, each coming faster and more painfully than the last. Writhing over the toy inside me—fighting against the agonizingly painful need of my next impending release—and gasping for air, a fleeting moan passes over my lips as the eighth release hits hard. It shoots through me like bolts of electricity. Isaac lets out a displeased groan behind me, and his thumb slides along the wand, the vibrations immediately increasing to an ungodly, painful speed. Cries of excruciating pleasure fill the room as he forces a quick ninth and tenth orgasm from me.

He turns off the wand, and I breathe a sigh of relief when it stops vibrating against my throbbing clit. After rising from behind me, Isaac steps before me and stares down at me, his face laced with disappointment as he tenderly swipes his thumb through a tear running down my cheek. Gripping my chin, he demands my stare. "I expect better tonight."

I nod silently for a second, struggling to catch my breath and find my voice. "Yes, Sir."

CHAPTER TEN
LIAM

"We've added how many new members?" I ask again in disbelief, hoping I misheard. While I don't know every one of our members by name, I am acutely aware that there are more than a handful of new faces striding through the doors tonight. Twenty-one by my count so far. Excluding the initial opening night, which was on a small scale, we've never added more than a dozen new members at a time.

"Sixty-one," Conor repeats the lofty number.

Tristan pours a Jameson from behind the bar and slides it to me. "Relax, Li," he urges. "Everyone was vetted, and we've run background checks on everyone. Not so much as a criminal complaint against any of them."

"And every new Dom came with personal recommendations of three other current members," Declan adds. "Should be smooth sailing."

Pouring a drink for Declan and then another for himself, Tristan shares, "Trust me, none of us want any of the type of issues that come with questionable members."

While I know this club is a large part of all our livelihoods, I can't shake the nagging feeling that adding this many new people on the same night is ludicrous. That many personalities in one room is too much of an unknown. There are only five of us. Even with our well-trained staff, it's far too many people for us to try to keep an eye on.

"No play tonight," I demand, immediately being met with grumblings from Finn and Conor.

"You're serious?" Finn huffs at his now-soiled plans for the evening.

"Very!" I twirl the glass in my hand against the white marble of the bar. "And watch your whiskey."

"I *always* watch my whiskey," Conor quips, tapping the bar for a refill.

Tristan holds the bottle of Jameson in his hand but hesitates to refill Conor's glass. Stowing the bottle behind the bar, Tristan laments, "Liam is right."

"Fuck!" Finn exclaims. "I expect it from the celibate bastard, but you, too?"

"Still not fucking celibate, Finn." I spin on my chair and stare at the sea of new faces before continuing, "The five of us need to keep watch tonight. We need to make sure that anyone indulging in play is doing so within the parameters of Risk-Aware Consensual Kink."

Something going wrong could ruin this for all of us.

Catlin approaches the five of us, and Finn pulls her into his lap. He places a soft kiss on the back of her shoulder. Nuzzling his chin into the crook of her neck as she gets comfortable, he sighs. "I'm not disagreeing with you, but next time, could you maybe say something a little earlier? Had I known this was going to be how the night went, I would've fucked this pretty wife of mine before we got here."

"Finn!" Cat squeals, her cheeks immediately turning a heated shade of blush.

Declan teases, "Sweetheart, while we can't see you when you're in the room at the end of the hall, from the sounds coming out of it, we all know the two of you aren't in there playing Monopoly."

Her discomfort only grows, and she drops her head to hide her face.

"Nothing to be embarrassed about. The people enjoying from the hallway go crazy listening to you come." Conor brushes his hand over the warmth of her cheek as the red hue adorably flares across her face. Dropping his voice to a whisper, he shares, "Fuck, *I* could get off simply listening to you come."

"*Piscín,*" Finn places a tender kiss on the side of her

neck as he wraps his hands around her waist. "Please get up so I can beat the piss out of my brother."

In turn, she wraps her hands over his and glances over her shoulder at Finn, "Let him dream, *mo ghrá*. Knowing he'll never have me is more torturous than your fist in his face."

"Fucking hell, Cat," Declan exclaims with voracious laughter, and the rest of us join in as Conor slinks back into his seat.

"The lot of you can deflate my hopes of enjoying these beautiful women you've all somehow convinced to love you," Conor playfully huffs, crossing his arms and pretending to sulk. "But just know, you can't take away the sweet dreams I have of Cat's little cotton panties or that sweet whimper Layla has right before her toes curl and she comes undone."

"Fuck it." Tristan's face heats with anger, quickly matching the same shade of Cat's embarrassment. "I don't care if this place is full of new members. *I'm* going to beat the fucking piss out of him."

"Can you all go one measly day without slugging each other?" Layla rolls her eyes as she approaches on Jorge's arm. "I think you have a bigger problem than the big guy wanting to fuck us all."

"She doesn't call me that because I'm tall." Conor winks at all of us, further aggravating Tristan.

"Keep telling yourself that," Layla teases, placing a kiss on his cheek. "Based on the line at valet, your new members are very eager to visit. Because I'm pretty sure every last one of them is waiting to get in."

"Fuck," I huff, sliding from my barstool. "Layla, sweetheart, join me on a trip to the viewing hall."

"Really?" Conor barks as she slips her hand into the crook of my arm. "I make a joke about sticking my dick in her and nearly get the piss beat out of me. Meanwhile, Liam asks to take her to the hall, and no one says a word?"

"You fucking twat." Declan rolls his eyes. "He's taking her with him so he doesn't look like a creepy bastard."

"Why?" Conor shrugs. "I wander the viewing hall on my own all the time."

"Exactly." I condescendingly pat his shoulder before walking from the bar with Layla.

CHAPTER ELEVEN

SASHA

All the time Isaac ranted about wanting to bring me to this club, I was expecting it to be like the places that Trevor used to take me. In our time together, we frequented many private dungeons. All of which looked a lot like low-budget BDSM porn sets with dark, dingy basements. Most with very questionable hygienic standards, or with a complete lack of standards based upon that one time Trevor tried to share me on some clearly soiled sheets.

The punishment I received was well worth not kneeling in some unknown guy's cum or having my face pressed into someone else's wet spot.

This place, though, is nothing like those dungeons. I never could have imagined that it would be like this. Everything about the lounge we're walking through is meticulous and opulent. The white marble floors are so spotless you could eat from them, and every chair is perfectly placed. Even the people match the atmosphere; everyone is dressed in well-fitted suits and cocktail dresses.

Suddenly feeling out of place, I glance down at the strappy, backless dress that Isaac insisted I wear tonight. My cleavage spills from the deep, swooping neckline of the almost-sheer black fabric. The hemline is so short that this dress should come with a complimentary Brazilian wax. Eyes keep falling to the still pink scars on my well-visible upper thigh, and the choice of this piece of fabric posing as a dress becomes obvious. *Isaac wants to show me off to everyone.*

Isaac presses his hand to the bare skin of my tailbone, and I startle at the unexpected touch. "You're sweating. Are you nervous, beautiful?" Isaac asks, oblivious—*or ignorant*—to the fact I'm clearly running a fever. Without waiting for a response, he leads me through the crowd toward the bar. "Maybe we should get you a drink to loosen you up a bit."

Pinning me between him and the bar, Isaac flags down the bartender. "Whiskey. Four doubles. Neat."

"I'm sorry, sir. We have drink limits. Two per patron and one at a time. Best I can do is a double for each of you," the bartender informs us as he shakes his head. Considering the handful of cold-and-flu medicine I took to make it through tonight, I don't really want a drink. Let alone two of them. *Not that I would tell Isaac no.*

"Fine," Isaac slides fifty dollars across the white marble bar with his Club Treskilion card. "Just don't be a stingy pour."

Collecting the money, the bartender tucks it into his pocket before responding, "I will be sure to give you the full two ounces, sir." I fight back my snicker and am happy that my back is to Isaac so he can't see the amusement I can't keep from spreading across my face. The bartender returns a moment later with two glasses and slides them across the bar before returning Isaac's card.

"To showing the best of Manhattan what a perfect girl you are for me." Isaac raises his glass and taps it against mine, sloshing the amber liquid in it. I mirror the small sip he takes from his glass, swallowing less than a shot, but his displeased eyes quickly tell me it's not enough. "Drink up. Our room will be ready in a few minutes, and you are too tense."

Lifting the glass, I swallow the rest of the warm, spicy liquid. A drop rolls over my chin as it burns down my throat. Placing a warm, wet kiss against my jaw, Isaac collects the droplet before grabbing his glass and leading me from the bar. We walk down a long black hallway, and Isaac hands me his glass. "Finish this for me, beautiful. I'm definitely more of a tequila man."

Knowing I can't handle this much alcohol in this short amount of time, I contemplate disobeying him or *accidentally* spilling the remaining shot from the glass in my hand. Thinking better of either of them—*and the punishment I know would ensue*—I lift the glass to my lips and swallow the shot.

After ushering me through the black decor of this side of the club, Isaac leads me to a hall at the far side. "Eyes down," he commands when we reach the roped entrance. "You are here to be watched, not to watch."

Dipping my head to honor his request, I stare at the back of his shoes as he walks through the crowded hallway. Stealing a glimpse as we pass a window, my eyes are drawn to the pleasure-filled face of a woman on the receiving end of a paddle. I'm so infatuated with her, I can't seem to stop staring as we pass, forcing me to lift my head to watch her take another strike.

Not once have I felt a glimmer of the euphoria on her face as any of the men I've played with have paddled me.

"This is our room." Isaac's voice ticks with excitement, and I drop my gaze back to the floor before he turns to find me disobeying him. He swipes his key card over the door handle, and the lock clicks open, granting us entry. I step into the room as Isaac pushes open the door, and I am in awe of how pristine it is. *Right down to the starched sheets.*

Decorative hooks adorn the entire wall. Hanging from them is every striking toy you could imagine. All of which I have ample experience with. *Some I wish I hadn't.* The room houses very little furniture—the freshly made bed, a leather couch, and a bondage bench similar to the one Isaac keeps in my punishment room.

Stepping behind me, Isaac pulls the thin strand of ribbon holding my tiny dress in place. It flutters to the floor, leaving me bare before the small crowd. The cold air wafts over my clammy body, chilling me to the core. Parting my lips to plead with Isaac to take me home, I find myself immediately silenced from the shock of him shoving a silicone gag into my mouth. Pressing my tongue against it, I try to shove it from my mouth as he wedges it behind my teeth and pumps the bulb to inflate it. And just like that, I can't talk back. *Or draw in a solid breath.*

"On the bench. Ass up." Feeling lightheaded, I hesitate to move. While I can barely keep my eyes open, I know Isaac is staring at me with disapproving annoyance. He steps close and tenderly cups my face before pushing the hair from my sweaty temple. He tucks it behind my ear as he leans close and darkly whispers, "I know you didn't want to come tonight, but if you're going to act like a disobedient brat, I'm going to be forced to treat you like one. Now, get your ass on the fucking bench."

Isaac wastes no time. The moment I'm secured to the bench, the crack of the paddle striking my backside echoes around the small room.

CHAPTER TWELVE

LIAM

With Layla on my arm, I walk from the lounge and into the club. No one bats an eye at the two of us until we head into the exhibition hall. That quickly draws some inquisitive looks from the regulars who know that I have my brother's woman nuzzled into my side. Submissives wander this hall with a man who isn't their Dom daily. And while I'm close with my sisters-in-law, the regulars know we aren't *that* close.

"No funny business," I tease, squeezing her hand in the crook of my arm as we step into the hall.

"No promises," Layla brats, glancing up at me with a wink. Placing her hand over mine, she asks, "In all seriousness, I know we aren't here for the same reason Tris and I visit, so what are we doing back here?"

Needing to grant myself a view through the window to our left, I nudge through the crowd until we're standing shoulder to shoulder before the pane of glass.

I pull Layla into me as she watches the couple engaged in a wax play scene. Wrapping my arms around her, I hold her closer than I should and whisper into her ear, "I want to make sure the new members are adhering to the rules of play—both in and out of the rooms—and having a gorgeous woman on my arm makes me a tad less conspicuous."

"Understood," she whispers. Slipping her hand into mine, she laces our fingers and plays along. "Show me all the things you want to do with me."

Layla continues to flirt and brat as we mingle among the other couples, making the ruse quite realistic. Like those surrounding us, we slowly walk the length of the hallway, pausing for a few minutes to admire the couples in various types of play on the other side of each window.

"Holy shit!" Layla exclaims, drawing both my attention and that of the couples beside us to the window on our right.

"What?" I squeeze her hand as my eyes dart around the room, looking for an issue with the woman bound to the Saint Andrew's cross. She appears to be perfectly fine. *Better than fine, actually*. From the euphoria on her face, it's quite clear she's deep in subspace.

"Sorry. It wasn't her that caught my attention. I've never seen anyone with that many piercings before," Layla whispers with a slight giggle, her eyes traveling up the Jacob's ladder studded through the shaft of the man standing a few feet before us.

"Next window, sweetheart, before your overt gawking gets us into trouble with your husband," I teasingly snark, pulling her from the glass. The two of us are still snickering when we reach the next window.

"Li." Layla's voice cracks, devoid of her prior jovialness, when she looks into the room. Following her distraught gaze, I find myself staring into the fear-filled, glassy brown eyes of a beautiful woman struggling to maintain consciousness. Her eyelids flutter, barely jarring open with the violent strikes of the leather-barbed flogger being swung by the inept tool behind her. A blueish hue tints her pouty pink lips, and her nostrils flare as she struggles to breathe.

Roughly rapping my knuckles against the window, I attempt to get his attention. He glances at me for a moment and proceeds to outright ignore me—and the clear distress of his partner—as he strikes her again.

"Open the fucking door!" I shout, driving my shoulder into it. The commotion draws the attention of the club as I slam into it a second time. The wood splinters, and it crashes into the room, with me staggering in behind it.

Continuing to ignore the woman bound to the bench, the asshole behind her spins to face me and barks, "This is an exhibition, not a fucking train."

"This is fucking over!" I snarl, fisting the front of his shirt. After pulling him toward me, I toss him across the room on his arse. I turn my attention to the bound woman in distress and grab at the bulb for the gag in her mouth. Twisting the release valve to deflate it, I run my fingers under her jaw and am relieved to find a faint pulse. My hand brushes against her overly warm skin as I swipe the sweat-matted hair from her face to remove the gag. When I remove the silicone plug that filled her mouth, spittle falls from her lips, but she doesn't take a breath. Layla works diligently to undo the restraints as I shout, "Call fucking 911. She isn't breathing."

Carefully wrapping my arms around her naked, lifeless body, I lift her from the bench and pull her into me. "She's mine," the fucking cunt who did this shouts, shoving himself from where I launched him and rushing toward me. "You don't get fucking touch he—"

Conor barrels into the room and grabs him by the throat, cutting his threat short. Slamming him into the wall, Conor's tone carries every ounce of anger I'm currently harboring. "No. *You* don't get to fucking touch her," he spits.

Kneeling on the cool marble tiles, I gently lay her at my feet. "Come on, sweetheart," I coax, grinding the butt of my palm against her sternum. Trying to revive her as I glare at the man in Conor's hold, I bark, "What's her fucking name?"

He stares back at me tight-lipped, and Conor plunges a fist into his gut to motivate him to speak. Painfully gasping for air, he exhales, "Sasha... Sasha Martin."

"C'mon, Sasha. Fucking breathe for me!" I plead. Pinching Sasha's nose and tipping her head back, I send two deep breaths into her mouth. I fill them twice more before rubbing over her chest again. *You don't deserve to die because of this piece of shit.* Bending down, I breathe for her again. When I pull back the third time, my warm breath sputters back against my lips, and Sasha's mouth flutters. *Thank fucking God.* Relief washes over me as she draws in a deep breath and it wafts over my face when she exhales.

"That's it. Breathe for me," I urge, staring down into her fear-filled eyes as she continues to take slow, deep breaths. Still groggy and confused, she gazes up at me through her heavy lids, and I soothe, "I've got you. You're safe, Sasha."

Swiftly pulling the sheet from the bed behind me, I haphazardly toss it over her body, attempting to provide her with a shred of modesty. Layla helps cover her as she kneels beside her with teary eyes of her own. Dusting my thumb over the trails of mascara, I tenderly rub Sasha's warm, ruddy cheeks while we wait for the ambulance.

Paramedics barge into the room, and the tool grunts in annoyance, "She's fucking fine. Tell these assholes you don't need to go to the hospital. Tell the—" Conor silences him, but it's too late. Sasha trembles and timidly nods as she tries to push from the floor. *Fuck, has he ever done a number on her...*

"Eyes on me, Sasha. He's leaving. You don't need to look at him again." I lightly cup her jaw and tip her face toward me, gently demanding her attention as Conor drags the source of her terror from the room. Sasha hesitantly meets my eyes, and I can feel her nerves as her pulse races against my fingertips. "We need to get you looked at. We need to make sure you're all right."

CHAPTER THIRTEEN

SASHA

"Okay," I softly sob, with fresh tears welling in my eyes.

The icy tiles press against my sweaty back, and I stare into the softest set of storm-blue eyes. They swirl with shades of blues and grays, like a sky fighting between a sunny day and torrential rain. The stranger continues to stroke my cheek and wipe away my tears—*showing me more tenderness than any of my Dominants*—as he continues to comfort me. "I've got you. I'll make sure you're okay."

I won't be okay.

The way Isaac looked at me a few minutes ago, I'm certain of it. The punishment for breaking my promise —for not being perfect—is going to be harsh. He will want to make sure I learn, so that I will do better for him next time.

"Ma'am, did you take anything?" the paramedic asks

as the other attaches a monitor to check my heart and provides a mask to help with my breathing.

The mask resting over my mouth muffles my answer. "No... I mean, just some medicine for my cold."

Still at my kneeling at my side, the stranger grits his jaw and exhales a seething breath at my response. "You're sick?" he asks angrily.

"I'm sorry," I mutter. "I don't want to get you, or anyone else, sick."

"Oh, sweetheart." He quietly sighs, reaching for my hand. His rigid demeanor doesn't match his gentle tone, and he gives me a light squeeze and rubs his thumb over the back of my palm. "Don't apologize. I'm not the least bit concerned about catching a cold."

The paramedics lift me onto a stretcher, and they start to wheel me from the room. Not letting go of my hand, the stranger walks alongside me through the now-empty club to the ambulance waiting in the valet section of the parking lot. As he opens the doors at the back of the ambulance, the paramedic says, "I'm sorry, but we can't allow you to ride with us unless you are family."

The stretcher jolts against the back of the rig as they prepare to lift me, and I'm hit with the realization that I'm going to the hospital. *I almost died.* My chest rattles, and tears stream down my cheeks as I sob uncontrollably. *Isaac was going to let me die.*

"You can write on your fucking paperwork that I'm her fucking grandmother for all I care," the stranger retorts, climbing into the back of the ambulance as they push my stretcher into it. Squeezing my hand as he takes a seat beside the stretcher, he proclaims, "I promised I'd make sure you're okay, and Evans don't break their promises."

"Thank you, Mr. Evans." I try to stifle my sobs.

"Liam," he corrects me. "Call me Liam."

———

After a barrage of tests, a slew of doctors, and some lofty concern about the welts on the back of my right thigh, the doctor informed me that everything looked good, but he'd like to keep my overnight for observation.

"You're a little fighter, aren't you?" Liam smirks when I toss against the mattress for the umpteenth time. Not wanting to be alone, I asked him to stay until I fell asleep. He promptly pulled a chair up to my bedside and has been sitting quietly beside me for the past hour while I fought against my fatigue. Brushing his hand over my blanket-covered shin, he adds, "Get some rest. You need it."

"What the fuck is going on in here?" Isaac barks from the doorway. Splatters of blood stain the front of his previously pristine, white Tom Ford shirt. There's a deep gash beneath his swollen and bruised left eye.

Storming into the room, he shoves Liam from my bedside. "She's mine."

"Yours?" Liam scoffs from the comfort of his chair.

"I fucking own her," Isaac spits, looming over Liam. "You think I'd let a little shit like you take her from me?"

"I've already put you on your arse once tonight. I have no qualms about doing it again," Liam warns.

"Get your shit, Sasha," Isaac demands. Terrified chills run down my spine when he tears the blanket from my legs and tosses it in Liam's face. "We're going home."

Rising from his seat with an eerie calmness, Liam spreads the blanket over the bed to cover my bare legs. "She isn't going *anywhere* with you."

"She's mine! *My* fucking sub. And if she knows what's good for her, she'll get her disobedient ass out of that fucking bed," Isaac snarls, reaching for me. His hand brushes my arm as Liam tears him away from my bedside.

Fisting the front of his shirt, Liam drives Isaac's back into the wall. He hits it with such force it causes the picture on the wall beside him to crash to the floor. "She's not fucking *yours*." Liam drives his forearm into Isaac's throat. "You don't fucking own her. And you sure as fuck don't treat her with the respect and admiration a submissive deserves."

Isaac's face grows a bright shade of crimson as Liam presses into his neck with the entire weight of his solid frame. He doesn't ease up, not even when the shade of Isaac's face begins to turn a blueish hue and as his nails tear at Liam's arm. I should be afraid. I should want to help him or at least feel some sort of anguish about what's happening to Isaac, but I don't. The only thing I feel is gratification, enjoying watching him pay his penance with the same terror I felt only a few hours ago.

"She nearly fucking died, and all you can think about is admonishing her for ruining *your* night." Liam drops his voice to a deep rumble. "You're nothing more than an abusive fuck"

Isaac struggles to breathe, and his fight falters from oxygen deprivation. He's turning blue and moments from death when Liam whispers, "If I see you anywhere near her or my club again, I'll fucking kill you."

CHAPTER FOURTEEN
LIAM

Pushing from the wall when I drop my arm, Isaac rasps, "Keep the fucking whore. She doesn't listen for shit anyway."

The room falls silent, except for the faint sound of Isaac barking at hospital staff as he makes his way toward the elevator at the end of the hall.

"I thought you were going to kill him," Sasha confides as Isaac storms from the room.

"I thought about it," I confess. One small shove and I could've crushed his trachea with my forearm. The world—*and Sasha*—would've been a better place for it.

"I wish you would have," she shares coldly, her pleading, chestnut eyes boring into mine.

Sasha rolls across the bed and onto her side, tucking the pillow into the crook of her neck. I pull the blanket up her body, silently encouraging her to get the rest she so desperately needs. Her sad, brown eyes meet mine. "He's not going to listen."

Grabbing my chair, I slide against the side of her bed and settle back into it to uphold my promise to her. We sit in silence, and I wait patiently as Sasha's eyelids grow heavy. She hovers on the brink of sleep and groggily mutters, "Isaac *always* gets what he wants. Money... Status... Me."

I should mind my business and definitely *not* say what's on my fucking mind. I should probably do a lot of things. Taking Sasha's hand, I give it a gentle squeeze and whisper, "Not this time, sweetheart."

From her bedside, I text my brothers.

> Where does this asshole live?

DECLAN

> You KNOW where Finn lives.

> I'm fucking serious. Where does he live?

CONOR

> I already beat the fucking piss out of him tonight

> Not good enough.

> He's still fucking breathing.

TRISTAN

> SoHo

> 7860 Mercer Street

I'll meet you there. Twenty minutes.

Pulling my card from my wallet, I tuck it into Sasha's hand before leaving her room. The traffic is so light at this hour that I make it from Midtown to SoHo in fifteen minutes. After parking my car down the block, I wait at the curb outside the next building for Tristan. He arrives a few minutes later and pulls his Tahoe into the alleyway between the two buildings.

"How's Layla?" I ask as we walk in silence into the building and to the small elevator bank, knowing how distraught she was over what transpired tonight.

We step into the empty cab when it arrives, and Tristan presses the button for the penthouse. "She's okay."

We ride in silence for a moment before I inform him, "Anyone that recommended this fuck is out. And whoever recommended them needs to be re-vetted. Because this shit isn't happening ever again."

"You'll get no argument from me about this." Tristan nods. "And I don't exactly see anyone but the rescinded members having an issue with it."

The elevator opens to a small foyer and the lone door to the penthouse. Tristan braces to shove his shoulder through it before I stop him. Pulling the lock pick from my pocket, I kneel to pop the door. "It's not going to look like an accident if we rip the door off the hinges."

"Apologies," Tristan quips with sarcasm. "I didn't realize we weren't going to beat him to death."

"He deserves to go out gasping for his last breath." I push open the unlocked door. Navigating through the dark, we make our way through his lavish apartment. Tristan and I both pause at a cracked bedroom door when we find him wanking in bed with his laptop on the bed beside him. Stepping into the room, I snark, "You're making this too fucking easy for me."

"Wh—what the fuck?" he blubbers with his hand still wrapped around his cock.

"Don't stop on our account," I tease as Tristan draws his gun to ensure Isaac stays exactly where he is. "This will be even more believable when they find you with a load crusted over your stomach."

"They?" Isaac squeaks.

I lift Isaac's discarded trousers from the floor as we cross the room, slipping the Gucci belt from the loops with every step. Standing beside his bed, I make a noose with the belt. "I know we listen and we don't judge." I overtly dart my eyes toward the laptop screen, drawing Tristan's attention to the snuff film. "But, what the actual fuck!"

"Does your mother know that's the shit you watch to get off?" Tristan asks.

Isaac snaps his head toward Tristan. "What?" he blusters.

Using the distraction to my advantage, I slip the noose over his head and quickly cinch it around his neck. I loop the loose end through the wrought iron headboard and pull it until Isaac gags. Leaning close, I can't help but torment him. As Isaac desperately tries to pull the restricting leather from his throat, I darkly whisper, "Tell me you're an abusive piece of shit and I'll tell my brother to shoot you in the head. Let you off easy."

He chokes on his words when I ever so slightly loosen the noose, his body craving the tiny breath over the confession that would save his life.

"Sorry," I taunt, pulling at the leather strap again. "I didn't quite catch that."

"You're a sick fuck sometimes," Tristan gaffs, taking a seat on the edge of the bed. "But by all means, do your thing."

Wavering between a suffocating hold and allowing him the faintest of breaths, I keep Isaac hovering at the terrifying edge of death for almost an hour and verbally berate him for being an inhumane piece of shit. He tastes death countless times, only to be repeatedly denied the relief of actually meeting his untimely end. Tears trickle down his face as he silently pleads for his life, his body so exhausted he can't even fight. "This time, I'm letting you feel exactly what you made Sasha go through." I pull the belt taut and his eyes blow wide, realizing that this is it. This is his end.

I knot the belt around the headboard when his body falls limp, leaving him to look like he had a tragic wanking accident. *Breath play is fucking dangerous.*

When we're riding the elevator back to the lobby, Tristan asks, "Feel better?"

"Yes." I nod before returning to our prior conversation. "No more mass member additions, either. And discreet panic buttons in the hall because my shoulder is fucking killing me."

"Poor baby," Tristan teases, reaching out to rub it before I smack his hand away. "And agreed."

Parting ways where Tristan parked his SUV, I walk down the block to mine. My phone buzzes, and I pull it from the front pocket of my jeans. Swiping it open, I find a text from Finn.

FINN

Fuck! Did I miss all the fun?

CHAPTER FIFTEEN
SASHA

After being provided with a clean bill of health and an appointment to make sure the hematomas on the back of my right thigh are healing properly, I'm discharged from the hospital shortly after food services served breakfast. I leave the hospital with nothing but the clothes on my back—*pale-green medical scrubs that don't belong to me*—and Liam Evans' business card.

I contemplated giving him a call this morning when I woke with his number tucked in my hand, but it didn't feel right. The amount of gratitude I want to give—for both saving my life and his sheer kindness—deserves more than an impersonal call.

The slightly oversized sneakers from the hospital's lost-and-found rub my sockless feet as I walk the ten blocks from the hospital, leaving my heels tender and irritated. At least the irritation is keeping my mind off how the cool spring breeze is nipping at my bare arms or blowing through the thin fabric.

When I reach my destination and pull open the door, I step into the warmth of the club. I vigorously rub my hands over my goose-pimpled arms to warm myself. The sleek, white lounge is as pristine this morning as it was last night. Only, unlike last night, there isn't a person to be seen. Still stroking my hands along my chilled skin, I tentatively walk down the black hallway toward the other side of the club. At the end of the hall, I call out, "Hello?"

"We aren't open yet," a confident and sweet woman's voice shouts from the bar.

"I...I'm sorry," I stammer. "The door was open. I was looking for Liam Evans."

"He ran out, but I can give him a call to see when he'll be back," a pretty—*and vaguely familiar looking*—petite brunette informs me, sliding from a stool at the bar.

"No." I shake my head. "I can come back another time."

She walks toward me with a broad and inviting smile. "Trust me, he will be more than happy to see you."

How does she know who I am? Everyone at this club would probably recognize me after last night.

"You really don't have to," I mutter as her fingers run over the screen of her cell phone. It dings a second later.

"Liam and Tristan are just down the block. They'll be here in a few minutes," she tells me, gesturing to a set of black leather chairs at a nearby table. We both take a seat. "I'm Layla, by the way."

"Sasha."

"I know." Layla fidgets slightly in her chair, staring at me with a tinge of bewilderment. "You look amazing after... everything. How are you feeling?"

I faintly remember her kneeling beside me and covering me with a sheet while Liam took care of me. "You were there," I blurt, ignoring her question.

Her smile fades slightly, and her eyes sadden. The air in the room suddenly feels thick and heavy. "Yes. I helped Liam get you..."

"Breathing?" I tease with an arched brow, trying desperately to lighten the suddenly grim mood.

Layla lets out a tiny chortle. "I was going to say, 'less blue,'" she retorts before slapping her hand over her mouth. "Shit, I'm sorry. That was fucking crass."

I like her.

"Don't be." I giggle awkwardly. "That shit was funny. Morbid, but funny."

A man bearing a resemblance to Liam joins us from the hallway with a warm smile. "The two of you seem to be having a good time."

"Oh, my coffee." Layla outstretches her hands toward the large, iced coffee he's carrying.

He pulls it back, keeping it from her grasp and winking. "I think you meant, 'Oh, love of my life.'"

"That's *exactly* what I said," she brats, reaching for the cup again. His lips purse, and he shakes his head, a disapproving look I know all too well. Isaac, Shawn, and Trevor would've left me unable to sit for days had I ever sassed them like her. I shift uncomfortably in my chair, waiting for him to punish her.

He runs his hand along her jaw and firmly grips her chin. Tipping her face up toward his, he leans down until their faces are inches apart. "You're such a fucking brat, *mo chuisle*. When I finish upstairs, I think you need a gentle reminder."

Dipping her playfully bashful face, she replies, "I think that is a good idea, Sir."

A sincere smile pulls at the corners of his mouth as he closes the distance to place an affectionate, wet kiss on her lips. Pulling back, he tenderly dusts his thumb along her lower lip as he hands her the coffee.

The men I've had in my life would've never.

"Thank you, baby," Layla purrs before taking a long sip of her iced beverage. Turning her attention to me, she introduces the two of us, "This is my husband, Tristan. And this is Sasha. She's waiting for Liam."

"Liam was dropping a case of Tullamore over at the pub. He should be here in a minute or two," Tristan explains. He outstretches his hand to shake mine, and I take it timidly. "Please excuse my rudeness, but I have several things to address before we open. It was nice to meet you, and I am truly sorry for what happened last night."

"Thank you."

Layla's brows furrow a little with concern. "In all seriousness, you're good?"

"Define good," I quip. "In the not-dead department, almost one hundred percent. Finding myself unemployed, homeless, and owning nothing but the borrowed clothes on my back… Yeah, that could probably be better."

"If I know anything about my husband and his brothers, they won't let you wind up on the street. I would bet my life on it." Layla closes her eyes and lets out a heavy exhale.

"She's right," Liam's familiar voice carries from the darkness of the hallway, startling me.

"I'll let the two of you…" Layla trails off as she stands from her chair.

Rising with her, I wrap my arms around her and squeeze her tightly, whispering, "Thank you."

CHAPTER SIXTEEN
LIAM

Knowing exactly where I was going after the hospital last night, it was reckless to leave Sasha with my business card. Yet, I couldn't help myself. Part of me hoped she would reach out so I knew she was okay. I never expected that she would show up at the club this morning, but I can't deny that I am happy to see her.

"My brothers and I will ensure you are taken care of." I reinforce the sincerity of what Layla and I are offering.

She shakes her head. "You don't have to do that."

"Yes. We do. While what happened to you could've happened anywhere—especially with *him*—it happened here. At Triskelion. We work really hard to ensure that men like Isaac don't have access to our club."

"I'm glad he did," Sasha softly confesses as she stares at me.

So am I. In ways that I can't quite put my finger on.

Looking down at her, I'm pleased to find her chestnut eyes are a bit more lively this morning. Even with the left one being surrounded by the crimson pool of a blown blood vessel, they harbor less anguish than they did last night. The mar in her eye—an unfortunate effect of asphyxiation—should heal within a week or two.

"If we had been at home, I wouldn't be here right now. It's actually why I'm here. Why I came to the club…" She fidgets uncomfortably as her gaze falls to the floor. "It doesn't seem like enough, but I wanted to say thank you."

"You don't need to thank me, sweetheart." I insist.

"I do." She sniffles, still staring down at our feet. She begins to ramble with her soft voice just barely above a whisper. "There were dozens of people in that hallway, but you were the only one who helped me. You stayed with me. How unbelievably kind you have been to me… And Isaac… All of what you did and… You really didn't have to."

"Yes. I did," I confide. Sliding my hand over her shoulder, I fight the urge to pull her into me. *There is something about her.* I want to wrap my arms around her—the need pulls at me like a compulsion—so I can protect her and give her what I know she so desperately needs.

"Why?" Her voice cracks, and her thoughts of unworthiness cut at my heart. No one deserves what she went through.

"I couldn't leave you like that." I should stop, and I shouldn't say any more, but the words continue to fall from my mouth. "I wouldn't have been able to live with myself knowing he ever had the opportunity to treat you—or *anyone*—like that ever again."

She shifts her weight, and her hands fidget at her thighs, struggling to find the confidence to say the words resting on the tip of her tongue. With a soft, timid tone, she asks, "Did he suffer?"

"Yes." I tenderly place the knuckle of my forefinger under her chin and pull her gaze up to me. "Does that upset you?"

"It should…" Sasha struggles to hold my gaze, pushing her chin against my finger to drop her face toward the floor. "I'm more upset that I thought he actually loved me. And hurt learning how little he cared about me."

Sitting in the empty club, Sasha and I talk for a couple of hours. The two of us quickly grow comfortable with each other, and our conversation centers on the club. "How long have you been in the lifestyle?" I ask.

"About eight years," she responds. *She was still a fucking baby.* "I grew up surrounded by very powerful men who pretty much always got what they wanted. For one of my brother's friends, that was me. He was my first Dom, and he taught me my role as a submissive."

"Do you enjoy submitting?"

"With him, I did." She glances at me before returning her stare to the cup of coffee between her hands on the table. Even with her face angled down, I can see a slight blush creeping over her cheeks as she continues, "He was rough and demanding, but not like the men after him. But I know they had to be because they were trying to teach me, and I couldn't learn otherwise."

"No, sweetheart." I wrap my hand over hers, shaking my head. "There is correction, and there is abuse. One stems from wanting to feel powerful. The other comes from a place of devotion and wanting a submissive to flourish."

I fucking hate how some of these men use the lifestyle as an excuse to do whatever they want.

"As a sadist, I enjoy watching my subs take my pain, but there are limits. You would learn that as my submissive."

My submissive?

With her long ash-brown hair, curvy figure, and angelic round face, it's impossible to deny how beautiful she is. Or how attracted to her I am. She is easily more stunning than the women I've been with recently, but she's also not my usual type.

Quite the opposite, actually.

I've had a long string of alpha-subs. Women who are strong and independent but enjoy giving over their full submission to me for a few months. Long enough to enjoy the dynamic, but short enough that I don't become too emotionally attached to them. Sasha is far too inexperienced in a proper D/s relationship to only spend a month or two with. She needs to be trained. Or, more correctly, retrained.

"Come stay with me." The words vomit from my mouth before I can stop them. As though I can't control myself—*or deny how much I want this*—they just keep coming. "You would learn a lot as my sub."

What the fuck are you doing, Liam?

CHAPTER SEVENTEEN
SASHA

"Be your submissive?" I timidly repeat his question before rebutting, "I barely know you."

It's not like not knowing a man's name has ever stopped them from taking your submission—or your body—before, Sasha.

There's something about Liam that isn't like all of them, though. He has shown me more compassion in the incredibly short time I've known him than any man I've ever met has. I can't believe how fast I dismissed him.

"I'm not asking as some ploy to take you home and fuck you." He pauses when I gasp at his bluntness. "I want to teach you, Sasha."

"Teach me?"

"You deserve to know how you should to be treated. I want to show you how amazingly powerful this lifestyle can really be. More than anything, I want to watch you grow."

I stare into the empty cup in my hands, trying to come up with a response.

"I'm not trying to push this on you." Liam reaches across the table and brushes the hair from my face. Glancing up, I'm met with the soft blue of his sincere eyes. "Tell me what you're thinking, or ask me a thousand questions if you have them. This is *your* decision."

My decision?

I haven't decided anything for myself my entire life. Father made them all when I was a little girl to ensure I was the perfect little princess for him. When he passed away, my brother took over for a while. Viktor, his best friend, quickly absolved him of my care when we started dating. I was seventeen. Then Alex... Trevor... Shawn... Isaac.

"I need to be clear that this would be temporary," Liam continues. "It would be an arrangement, not the beginning of a long-term relationship. I would be your teacher, and you would be my student. During our time together, I would be fully committed to you and your training."

"How temporary?"

Liam mulls over my question, taking a moment to answer, "Six months."

"Would you have another sub, too?" I ask, assuming he would want to have someone else to take care of his needs.

"Just you," he tries to calm the inquisitive look taking over my face. "During our six months, I would be fully committed to you. *Only* you. Completely monogamous."

"Monogamous?" My brows furrow with confusion, leaving me inadvertently mocking the look on his face. "I thought you said you didn't want to have sex with me?"

"I didn't say I don't want to have sex with you, sweetheart," he quickly refutes, a gentle chuckle rattling in his chest. "I said this wasn't a ploy to take you home to fuck you. You are fucking gorgeous. I would eagerly fuck you. But I'll earn your desire as I earn your submission. And when I do, I will enjoy every inch of your beautiful body."

I swallow hard, and I swear the sound of my gulp echoes through the empty club as a heated flush rises up my neck and over my cheeks. His overtness makes it hard to maintain his searing gaze, and I drop my eyes to the table again. I shift in my seat, trying to relief some of my emotional discomfort with the physical sensation. The movement leaves me suddenly acutely aware of the wound below my butt. "Will you punish me?" I blurt.

"No." Liam shakes his head. "When you don't adhere to our rules, I will correct you."

"Will it hurt?"

"Yes. Sometimes," he answers honestly. "I will hurt you, but I will *never* harm you."

It feels like each question I ask leads to another, but Liam answers every last one. Running his hand over mine, he insists, "This is your decision. One you don't need to make today. I will have Layla book a hotel for you until we can find you a suitable place to stay for a while."

I'm either quickly growing comfortable with this idea, or Liam is working some magical reverse psychology on me. Every time he offers me time and space, I lean closer to blindly accepting his offer.

"I'm not saying that I am, but if I were to say yes, what would I call you?"

"Liam."

"Not Sir? King? Lord? Or Master?"

"Liam," he repeats. "I will earn the privilege of an honorific."

———

As promised, Liam gave me a place to stay for the night. A small suite at the luxurious Dominick Hotel.

After enjoying the largest whirlpool tub I've ever had the privilege of soaking in. I am eating a cheeseburger and french fries from room service in the fluffy terry hotel robe when I am surprised by a knock at the door. Opening it, I find the bellhop with several shopping bags. He hands me the bags and a black envelope with gold foiling.

"I'm sorry, but I don't have any money for a tip."

"It's already been taken care of, ma'am," the bellhop informs me.

After closing the door, I place the bags at the foot of the bed and open the envelope.

Layla helped me guess your size, but I thought you would appreciate having more to wear than those scrubs or a hotel robe.
—Liam

He apparently has no idea how amazing this bathrobe is.

When I open the first bag, I find out a pair of leggings, a fitted T-shirt, and a long, thin sweater. The next bag contains three identical pairs of booties in different sizes. *Definitely covering all his bases.* Reaching into the third bag, a tiny gasp falls from my lips. Pulling my hand out of it, I have a fistful of lacy panties and an equally sheer bra dangling from the strap.

God, I hope Layla picked these out.

Hastily, I shove the panties back into the bag, and I move everything to the settee under the window. Removing the robe and tossing it on the end of the bed, I climb between soft linen sheets and flip on the TV. I stare mindlessly at the screen for an hour before realizing that I'm so consumed by my thoughts that I have no idea what is happening between the characters.

Maybe a good night's sleep will clear my mind so that I can make this decision.

Eventually turning off the TV, I get comfortable in the bed. Only sleep isn't forthcoming. Instead of the inside of my eyelids, I find myself flitting between staring at the ceiling and the bedside alarm clock until 3:00 a.m. The glow of the alarm clock glimmers on the foil of Liam's business card resting on the nightstand. Grabbing the card, I turn it over in my hand for a few minutes.

Fuck it.

Without allowing myself to overthink it, I flip on the sconce beside the bed. I lift the receiver from the base of the phone and dial the number on the card. It rings once before Liam answers, "Are you okay, Sasha?"

"Yes," I reply. "How did you know it was me?"

"Good guess... and caller ID," he teases.

"It's very late. Why aren't you sleeping?"

"I can't." I sigh heavily. "I've been up all night thinking about your offer."

"Like I said in the club, you don't have to make a decision right now."

Taking a deep breath, I blow it out slowly before giving him the answer that has been weighing on me all night. "Okay."

"We can talk about it more tomorrow."

"No… I mean… I'm saying yes," I clarify. "I want to accept your offer of training."

"Good." His tone carries a glimmer of delight, and I can't help but smile. "Now, be a good girl and get some sleep. I'll be at the hotel to pick you up at 10:00 a.m. Good night, sweetheart."

"Night, Liam."

CHAPTER EIGHTEEN

LIAM

Preparations for Sasha to move into my apartment started the moment she left the club for the Dominick. Actually, they started before that. The moment she let her curiosity show, I knew she was going to say yes.

I just didn't expect it to be so soon.

Taking my own advice, I flip off the light in the spare bedroom and head down the hall to mine. I set an alarm to ensure I have adequate time to get to her hotel by 10:00 a.m.

Keeping busy getting ready for Sasha's anticipated arrival stopped me from thinking about my impulsivity this evening, but with my head resting on the soft, down pillow, it's suddenly the only thing I can think about.

Untrained.

She's had horrible examples of Dominants. Training her will be like teaching a new submissive.

Untested.

We have not played together, and I have no idea if we are compatible. The way I lead and the things I like might not be compatible with how she learns to follow. We might not be a good fit for a training dynamic.

Unknown.

The two of us are practically strangers, and she's moving in this morning. Several women have lived here over the years. All of them were trained—*very well-trained*—and appropriately tested long before an offer was extended to be their Dom or provide them with a key to my apartment.

I don't know what's more ridiculous... The fact that I offered my dominance to Sasha. Or lengths I was willing to go to ensure she accepted it.

———

My alarm blares, and I'm surprised to find that I actually managed to get a few hours of sleep. After a quick shower, I get dressed and send a quick text to my brothers before heading down to the parking garage.

Won't be coming to the club today, taking care of Sasha.

CONOR

I bet you will be TAKING CARE of her

FINN

Do you even remember how sex works
at his point?

Or do you need one of us to draw you
a picture?

Fuck the lot of you.

TRISTAN

Layla will be there in about an hour.

She has a key, so she can let herself in.

FINN

Sasha AND Layla. Is Tris sharing
again?

CONOR

Please say yes!

Just one picture of Layla with Sasha
between her thighs…

Or Layla between Sasha's. I'm not
picky.

DECLAN

Pretty sure if you keep at it, you're
going to need ice for the fat lip Tris is
going to give you when he gets to the
club.

TRISTAN

Conor, I literally have one word for you:
TINDER

Shoving the phone into my jacket pocket with a
laugh, I slide into the driver's seat and turn over the

engine. The display illuminates, and I note the time. *9:15 a.m.*

Here's to hoping traffic isn't fucking horrendous.

I pull into the valet with around eight minutes to spare. The attendant takes my keys, and I head inside, aiming for the elevator bank. I am surprised to find Sasha stepping from the elevator cab and into the lobby. The clothes Layla chose fit her impeccably. The long open-front sweater provides a modest view of the leggings hugging the generous curves of her hips and thighs, and the V-neck of her well-fitted T-shirt provides the faintest peek at the cleavage of her ample breasts.

Walking toward me—struggling to carry all the bags I had delivered yesterday—she flashes a short, nervous smile. "Good morning, beautiful," I greet her, watching her shoulders drop and her face crumble as the words pass my lips. "Is it my arrival or the name that makes you uncomfortable?"

Her eyes widen, clearly surprised by my observation, and she whispers, "Beautiful... That was Isaac's name for me."

"You are far too stunning for me not to compliment your appearance, but I will be mindful of using that word," I promise, reaching for the bags to relieve her of their weight. "What are you doing in the lobby?"

"Coming to meet you," she answers timidly. "So you don't have to wait for me."

"I appreciate your punctuality, but I will *always* come to collect you," I explain. "I don't want you going anywhere without me or protection."

"I...I'm sorry," she stammers.

"And most of all"—I collect the last bag from her hand—"I need you to let me take care of you. Understood?"

Struggling to meet my gaze, Sasha nods her agreement.

"I'm not angry or upset with you, sweetheart," I assure her, noting her disappointment in her own behavior.

"Really?" She sounds genuinely surprised as we walk to my car, which is still sitting in the valet.

I deal with the attendant and retrieve my keys, delaying my answer to her. "Yes, really." I open her car door, and she lifts a black folder from the passenger seat to climb into it. "Why don't we go get some brunch before I take you to my place? It'll give us a chance to discuss the contract in your hands."

Closing her door, I stow her bags in the trunk. I join her in the car and drive toward the Williamsburg Bridge, heading into Brooklyn. It's thirty minutes in the opposite direction of my apartment, but The Galway has a remarkable traditional Irish breakfast, right down to the beans and soda bread.

This late in the morning, the restaurant is sparsely populated, and it only takes a few minutes for us to get a large semi-circle booth and a couple of cups of coffee.

I order for us both—after Sasha vehemently denies being hungry—waiting for the server to leave before sliding along the hunter-green leather bench to sit closer to her. Placing the folder between the two of us on the table, I open it to reveal the contract within.

CHAPTER NINETEEN

SASHA

Liam sits so close that I inhale the faint spicy oak of his cologne as I stare down at the open folder he splayed across the table. My eyes are drawn to the large, bold letters at the top of the paper. Staring at the title, my tone is laced with curiosity when I mumble, "A contract?"

"Yes," he answers flatly. "This goes far beyond detailing the length of our arrangement. Communication between us is absolutely vital—more so than a traditional relationship—and this walks us both through that conversation. I want you to know in explicit detail what I'm offering *to* you and what I am going to require *of* you. This will also make sure I know what you need from *me*."

From talking to him yesterday, I knew Liam was going to be completely different from the other men I've been with, but this is vastly uncharted territory for me. *What I need?* It has been ingrained in me that my job as a submissive is to make sure my Dom's needs are met. It has never been about my desires.

"What we decide today isn't concrete," he continues, pulling me from my thoughts. "We can always renegotiate rules and limits as our relationship develops."

My eyes roam down the contract. Beneath the six-month term of our arrangement are bullet points of his rules for me.

THE SUBMISSIVE:

-WILL FOLLOW COMMANDS IN AN APPROPRIATE MANNER AND TIMEFRAME

-WILL MAKE EYE CONTACT WHEN BEING SPOKEN TO OR SPEAKING

-WILL EAT THREE MEALS A DAY AND DRINK A MINIMUM OF FIVE GLASSES OF WATER

-WILL NEVER HIDE THEIR FEELINGS OR THOUGHTS

-WILL MAINTAIN PRIDE IN HER DRESS, APPEARANCE, AND HYGIENE (TO INCLUDE REMAINING HAIR-FREE AT ALL TIMES)

-WILL INFORM THE DOMINANT IF THEY ARE TOO UNWELL (PHYSICALLY OR MENTALLY) FOR SEXUAL ACTIVITY

-WILL NOT SEEK SEXUAL GRATIFICATION WITHOUT PERMISSION

-WILL THANK HER DOMINANT FOR ALL ORGASMS HE PROVIDES OR ALLOWS

-WILL ACCEPT ALL CORRECTIVE DISCIPLINE, UNDERSTANDING IT IS OUT OF CARE, LOVE, AND FOR PERSONAL GROWTH

-WILL ADDRESS THE DOMINANT BY THEIR CHOSEN HONORIFIC AS DIRECTED

-WILL NOT LEAVE HOME WITHOUT DOMINANT'S PERMISSION

-WILL NOT ABUSE THEIR USE OF TRAFFIC LIGHT SAFEWORDS (YELLOW AND RED), ONLY UTILIZING THEM WHEN THEY FEEL THEIR PERSONAL SAFETY (PHYSICAL OR MENTAL) IS COMPROMISED

-WILL PERFORM SEXUAL ACTS WHEN AND HOW THE DOMINANT DEEMS FIT

"Are those reasonable to you?" Liam asks. "Do you think you will be able to follow them?"

My eyes glossing over them once more, I reply, "Yes."

Liam's fingers dust along cheek, pulling my chin and forcing my attention from the paper to him. "Then I expect you to look at me when you answer."

Meeting his caring—yet authoritative—gaze, I stare into the warmth of his stormy blue eyes and repeat, "Yes."

"That's better. Good girl." His fingertips slide from my jaw with a feathery touch. My heart flutters, and I'm not sure if it's from the praise or the feel of his skin on mine.

The server returns with our food, and we eat breakfast as we discuss a checklist of items and activities. He patiently takes his time explaining the ones that I don't know, allowing me to provide him with a well-informed answer. By the time we finish, the list is riddled with notes regarding things I have expressed enjoyment in and my aversion to others.

"Almost done," Liam informs me, flipping the page. My brows furrow when it isn't more activities or rules for me but rules for him.

THE DOMINANT:

-WILL TAKE RESPONSIBILITY FOR THE CARE (PHYSICAL AND MENTAL), PROPER TRAINING, CORRECTION, AND GUIDANCE OF THE SUBMISSIVE

-WILL NOT GIVE THE SUBMISSIVE TO OR COMMAND THE SUBMISSIVE TO PERFORM ACTS OF SERVICE (SEXUAL OR OTHERWISE) TO/FOR OTHER DOMINANTS

-WILL PROVIDE A SAFE ENVIRONMENT, ENSURING NOT TO INJURE THE SUBMISSIVE PHYSICALLY OR MENTALLY

-WILL OBTAIN CONSENT PRIOR TO LEAVING ANY PERMANENT MARKS ON THE SUBMISSIVE

-WILL NEVER PROVIDE CORRECTIVE DISCIPLINE IN ANGER

-WILL ACKNOWLEDGE SUBMISSIVE'S USE OF SAFEWORDS WITHOUT FAIL, IMMEDIATELY ENDING ANY ACT BEING PERFORMED

-WILL MAINTAIN RISK-AWARE CONSENSUAL KINK IS ADHERED TO AT ALL TIMES

I read his list of rules no less than five times from start to finish. My thoughts drifting to the treatment in my prior relationships... Being commanded to please other men or women... The things Trevor, Shawn, or Isaac would do to me when they came home after a bad day, or I upset them by breaking a rule... Isaac's name is carved into my thigh.

Liam lifts a pen from the table and adds to the neatly typed list

will not address submissive as 'beautiful' or any other name deemed to elicit negative emotions from prior partners

I'm overwhelmed with what he is promising me, and how aware he is of my feelings, that tears well in my eyes. I blink rapidly, unsuccessfully trying to keep them at bay, but they begin to trickle down my cheeks. Liam cups my face, and his thumbs tenderly wipe away each tear as he look sat me with heartfelt concern. "Why are you crying, sweetheart?"

"I... No one... You..." I stammer, trying not to open the floodgate of emotions he's drawing from me.

"It's okay. I understand," he whispers when I can't find my words. "I'm sorry that other men haven't given you the decency listed on that paper."

Using his gentle hold on my face, he pulls me closer and presses his soft, warm lips to my forehead. "You deserve better, and I'm going to make sure you learn that."

CHAPTER TWENTY
LIAM

Rubbing my thumbs over her now-reddened cheeks, I wipe away Sasha's tears before grabbing a napkin to dry her face. I exude the softness that she needs, but beneath the surface, heated rage is coursing through my veins. My thoughts race with visions of eliminating the men who had the audacity to treat her the way they did. And realizing that I let Isaac off way too fucking easy.

While Sasha and I haven't delved into her past—*I'll earn her trust first*—it is beyond apparent that they all sorely mistreated her. The list of my rules should be the bare minimum behavior of any Dominant.

Period. No discourse needed.

All of them are responsible for her coming so close to dying a couple of nights ago in my club. Each of them put her beneath their needs and desires—ingraining poor information about my world and this lifestyle—

until she was so fragile that she wound up with a man like Isaac. All of them deserve to pay for that.

And they will…

"I'm sorry," Sasha inhales, embarrassed about the current state of her emotions. Half joking, she blurts, "I'm broken."

"Don't say that," I admonish before taking her hand and giving it a gentle squeeze. "You're not broken, Sasha. You're hurt, and I'm going to help heal you."

Staring at the delicate woman before me, I am met with the reality of how much work she's going to need as my student. This is no longer about an overwhelming protective desire to teach her about this world. It's so much more. I am determined to watch her grow. To fucking flourish. By the time she leaves me, I want her to be a powerhouse. A strong, confident sub that willfully gives her submission to a Dominant who earns it and is grateful for the gift she's bestowing upon them when she kneels at their feet.

For the gift she is temporarily giving me.

My phone buzzes a few times against the dark mahogany of the table, and I flip it over to see a text message from Layla.

LAYLA

All set, Li.

> It might be good to ease her into all of us before family dinner on Sunday. If she wants, I'd love to get together with her this week for lunch.

If that isn't the fucking truth...

> All of us would.

"Layla is wondering if you would like to go to lunch this week with her and my sisters-in-law," I inform Sasha. "I'm going to tell her yes for you. I think it would be good for you to have confidants. Other women who will understand what we're doing and be more than open to talking with you about their experiences."

"Okay," she responds, nodding nervously.

Swiping my thumbs across the phone, I send my reply.

> Definitely. Thank you.

> Please also take her shopping for anything she needs.

> Shopping. I guess... If I have to

After paying the check and walking to the car, we begin the near-hour-long drive to my apartment. Free from the earshot of others, I disclose, "If you're going to be a part of my life for the next six months, there is something that I feel is important to share with you."

Sasha shifts her weight, the black leather of the seat crinkling beneath her as she turns to face me. *Good fucking girl.* She hesitates for a moment and trepidatiously asks, "What is it?"

"My brothers and I, we do more than run the club." I pause for a second to gauge her reaction. "We have another *business* that puts us—*and you*—at risk."

With a tiny nod, she confesses, "I know."

"You know?" I ask with a shock-laced tone.

Sasha lets out a tiny giggle, teasing, "It's not exactly a secret who the Evans brothers are." While I do not appreciate her tone and the bit of brattiness it has, I am so pleased to see a bit of her personality that I let it slide.

"Knowing that and so little else about me, why did you agree to let me train you?" I ask with genuine curiosity.

"You have been nothing but kind and compassionate to me since the moment I met you." She gives a little shrug of her shoulders. "And Layla and, sort of, Tristan."

I glance from the road to her with an arched brow, silently urging her to expand on her admission. When she doesn't, I encourage, "Go on."

"Layla confirmed what I thought, that you have a good heart. And your brother... It was the way he treated her when she was bratting him. He didn't get upset or hit her. He just informed her a correction was coming, which she accepted willingly."

"That's their thing," I explain, turning my attention back to the road. "He likes her brattiness because he enjoys putting her back into her place."

"And you?"

"I am surrounded by brothers' brats—who I love dearly—but I do not desire to have one of my own."

The final blocks of our drive are taken in silence, with Sasha staring out the window as I drive through Lincoln Square. Passing the grassy oasis before my building, she gasps, "You live here?"

"For the time being, so do you." I smirk, pulling into the parking garage and navigating the levels to my designated spot. We take the elevator up to my floor. She steps from the cab when the doors open, glancing between the two doors—mine and the one for the apartment that faces the city. I place my hand on the small of her back and lead her toward mine. Swiping my phone over the lock, I push open the door and usher her inside.

"Welcome home, Sasha."

CHAPTER TWENTY-ONE

SASHA

Stepping into Liam's apartment, I slowly exhale, "Wow."

It's remarkable.

My eyes dart around the grand space, trying to take it all in. The palette is rich with shades of brown and gray, with the perfect amount of cream fixtures and furnishings to keep it from feeling too dark. The heels of my new booties click against the hardwood floor as I walk toward the massive, double-sided, marble fireplace in the center of the room.

The same gray stone adorns the counters of the dark-gray kitchen at the far end of the open space. It is massive, with an island big enough to host a party—or his family. The island and counters are immaculate, with cooking utensils, oils, and seasonings perfectly arranged in decorative canisters. "You like to cook?" I ask.

"No." His answer surprises me. "The only things I use in here are the microwave for takeout leftovers and the dishwasher."

"A kitchen like that and you don't cook?" I laugh. "That's the kind of kitchen I dream of."

"If you enjoy cooking, you are welcome to it. I will happily eat a meal that doesn't come from Happy Fortune down the street."

Continuing to wander the space as Liam locks the door and empties his pockets onto the table in the small foyer. I run my hands along the soft brown leather couch as I make my way toward the floor-to-ceiling windows. Staring over the terrace, I take in the waterfront view. Liam's reflection alerts me that he is standing immediately behind me. "The sunsets are fucking breathtaking. Nearly as gorgeous as you," he flirtatiously whispers, causing my cheeks to flush. "Let me show you the rest of the place."

Leading me through the apartment, Liam shows me his office and a small home gym. We reach the end of the hallway, and Liam points at each of the doors. "The one on the right is my room, and the one on the left is yours."

Taken back, I spin toward him and ask, "I won't be in your room?"

"I told you, sweetheart, this wasn't a rouse to merely fuck you."

"When I agreed, I just assumed—"

With a firm tone, he imparts, "You will sleep in your own bed."

"Oh..." I blurt, realizing a second too late it sounds like I'm all but begging for him to fuck me. Not that the thought hasn't crossed my mind at least a couple of dozen times with our conversations being focused on sex at the restaurant.

"I only share my bed with women I'm in relationships with. Not ones I'm training." Reaching around me, he turns the knob to the door for my room and pushes it open. "It keeps the emotional boundaries clear, so that when this arrangement comes to an end neither of us is expecting more. You will be sleeping in here."

Lightly gripping my shoulders, he turns me toward the open threshold, and I am in awe of the room before me. It has the same sensational view of the water as the living room. The walls are a deep gray like the rest of the apartment, but the linens and decor are feminine shades of dusty rose and ultra-pale pink. A vase of fresh flowers to match the duvet sits on the center of the dresser.

"You did all this for me?" I exclaim.

"I had some help," he shares, walking into the room. "Layla helped to choose the bedding and bought you some more clothes."

Crossing the room, I excitedly pull open the closet door and am met with a near-full closet. I flip through the hangars to see them better, loving everything that Layla got for me. "I assumed since you didn't reach out about what I sent last night that everything we had got was the right size."

"It was."

"When you have lunch with Layla, Cat, and Quinn later this week, I'll be sure to give you my card so you can buy yourself some other things you like."

His generosity is overwhelming, and as much as I appreciate and like it, it makes me feel uncomfortable. Dropping my gaze to the floor, I mutter, "You really didn't have to do all this for me."

"I will let this one slide, and I will give you the rest of the night to get comfortable here before enforcing the rest of the rules." Liam grips my chin and pulls my gaze back up to him. With a deep tone, he firmly instructs, "But from this moment onward, you will look at me when you speak and when you are spoken to. Understood?"

"Yes."

"And do you know why?"

Afraid I'm going to give the wrong answer, my lower lip quivers and my voice cracks when I respond, "Because it's a rule, and you told me to."

"No." Liam shakes his head. "Every bit of your submission belongs to me now. Other men do not get to hold that kind of power of you. You will look me in the eye so you develop the ability to stand toe-to-toe with *any* man and stare them in the eye when you speak."

"I understand." *But I don't.* He is the only man I have ever met who wants that. Shawn wanted me to bow for him; he liked me weak and timid. Isaac made certain I learned to be quiet unless spoken to, and even then, to only answer in ways he approved of. Even my father always made sure I knew my place: quiet and out of sight unless requested to be present.

"You will learn to be confident as my submissive," Liam insists. "And we start your training tomorrow."

CHAPTER TWENTY-TWO

LIAM

Stepping from a post-workout shower, I'm overwhelmed with the delectable aroma of whatever Sasha is making for dinner. Her cooking ability was unexpected but a remarkable perk to our arrangement.

"What's for dinner," I call, walking down the hall toward the kitchen with my shirt in hand. When she turns around to answer me, her eyes drop to my bare chest. They rake down my chest to my abs, and her mouth slowly falls open with every inch. Pulling my T-shirt over my head as I approach her, I tease. "Are you drooling over the amazing smells coming from this kitchen or me?"

"Both," she exhales before facing the stove, trying to hide the undeniable look of lust in her eyes. We have spent nearly every waking moment of the past three days together, and there is undeniably a physical attraction between us. I've caught her eyes lingering on me on more than one occasion, and I sure as fuck have been thinking about her.

Usually, my submissive moves in after we've established our dynamic and we're already intimate. As much as I want to touch Sasha—*actually* **touch** *her*—I also want there to be some semblance of comfort and trust between us first. I just didn't realize how fucking unbearable waiting for that would be.

Sliding my hand down her back and slowly through the dimple above her arse, I hook it over the curve of her hip and ask, "So, what's for dinner?"

You? Because I'm fucking starving.

"Spaghetti Bolognese." She crooks her neck to glance at me over her shoulder to answer, continuing to stir the sauce on the stove. Letting her finish, I pour two glasses from the bottle of Merlot she used to make dinner. I place them both on the island and grab silverware while she plates our meal. Taking seats beside each other, we eat at the island.

"That was fucking delicious," I praise again when we finish. Rising from her barstool, she grabs my plate, and I wrap my hand over it to stop her. "I've got it. I'll clean this up."

"Are you sure?" she asks, her eyes drifting from me to the pile of pots and pans in the kitchen sink and sauce splatters on the countertop.

"Yes. I am." Grabbing our plates, I place them into the sink before returning to her. "You worked very hard on this for me. I want to make sure you know I appreciate it. I will clean up."

"I like cooking for you but thank you."

"While I take care of this, I want you to take care of *you*." Tucking her hair behind her ear, I softly insist, "I want you to go take a shower to relax. I'll be on the couch when you're done."

I take a seat on the couch after finishing the dishes, wondering how we've fallen into a rhythm and comfortability which each other so quickly. A few minutes later, Sasha returns from her shower. Her ash-brown hair, still damp, darkens the front of her camisole where it has dripped onto the fabric. Beneath it, her breasts bounce with every step she takes in my direction. Unable to tear my eyes from her, I feel beside me for a cushion and drop it to the floor between my feet. Gesturing to the pillow, I instruct, "Please kneel for me." She looks between me and the floor a few times, draws a slow breath, and falls to her knees between my feet.

"Straighten up and shoulders back," I correct, watching her posture improve. "There are two different commands I will give when I ask you to kneel for me: kneel and admire."

Her throat bobs, and she gives a nod, acknowledging her understanding. "Kneel is for both play and when I need you to await correction. I expect this posture from you, your hands on your thighs and your head bowed to the floor. Show me."

We have been working our way through various standing and floor positions. I am teaching her my terms, how to correctly present herself in each of them, and slowly working them into our lives. Eventually, they will be second nature, and she will comply perfectly without question or hesitation.

"Good girl," I praise, appreciating how she maintains her posture with her head bowed and how still she is as she awaits my next command. "In the future, kneel will not come with the comforts of the pillow beneath your knees."

She is a remarkable student.

"When I instruct you to admire, I will provide you with a cushion. You will kneel at my feet, place your arms on my legs, and lift your head." She follows my final instruction and tentatively rests her elbows on my knees. Grabbing her hands, I adjust each of her arms so that they run the length of my thighs. This position puts her face and breasts on display for me. Brushing her damp hair from her face, I tuck it behind her ear and marvel at her beauty.

Her eyes reflect the glow of the full moon shining through the windows behind me, and in this light, I first notice the tiny flecks of green around her iris. The natural rosiness of her cheeks slowly begins to burn as she grows uncomfortable with the passing minutes of my admiration. *I could stare at her for hours.* "This position allows me the pleasure of looking at you."

Or to let her worship my cock with her mouth.

My cock twitches at the thought of being taken between her lips and over the slickness of her tongue as she slides me down her throat. Sasha drags her tongue along her lower lip, and I can't help but wonder if she is thinking also about swallowing my cock. I press my thumb to her lips, and she leans her cheek toward my palm, seeking my touch. Trailing my thumb through the wetness on her lips, I ask, "Do you want my touch?"

"Yes." Her quickly delivered answer is drawn out and breathy.

She doesn't just want my touch. She needs to be touched.

"I need you to trust me before I fuck you the way I truly want to. I will be much less rough than I prefer this time, but I will not be gentle," I inform her. "Knowing that, are you sure?"

"Yes."

CHAPTER TWENTY-THREE
SASHA

Liam grips my chin and bends his face toward me. Denying me his kiss, his perfectly manicured stubble drags along my cheek until his lips are resting against my ear. His warm breath blows against the side of my face. "Stand." His command is a deep, gravelly whisper. The rich vibrations of his demand against my skin travel straight to my pussy, causing it to flutter and my breath to hitch as I rush to rise to my feet.

"Take off your pants," he instructs. His eyes roll over my body, watching my every move intently. I pull at the drawstring of my silk pajama bottoms and let them fall to the floor. I step from the pool of silk around my feet and lightly kick them across the floor. Standing before him in nothing but my sheer pink thong and matching cotton camisole, his heated gaze rakes over me. "*Taibhseach*. You are fucking gorgeous."

He stares at me hungrily, and my heart races in my chest as I impatiently await his next command. "On my lap," he directs, and I climb until I am straddling him. Gripping my ass so hard that his fingers dimple the skin, he yanks me over one thigh and drags me toward his hip. The movement is so quick and deliberate that I'm still gasping when he releases my cheek.

"Ride it," he gruffly demands. While I understand what he's asking, the foreignness of his command causes me to pause. Liam's hand slaps against my ass, and a started yelp flies from my lungs. The burn of his strike radiates across my skin so clearly I can feel his handprint after he removes his palm. "Ride my thigh like you'd ride my fucking cock."

Moving my hips, I mimic the motion of riding over his cock. He flexes his leg, and the ridges of his thick, muscular thigh rub against my clit with every movement of my hips. His large hand roughly grips my ass cheek, and he forces me to set a pace and friction that quickly has me panting and on the brink.

"That's it," he coaxes. I love how he's praised me throughout my training so far, but hearing it when I'm on the verge affects me much more strongly. *I could do anything with him urging me on.* "You're going to ride me just like that until I tell you to stop. I'm going to watch as you make yourself repeatedly come all over me until you're so fucking soaked that I can slip my fat cock into you with ease."

Gripping my wrist, Liam pulls my hand to the growing bulge in his pants. He presses my palm against him, moaning as he slides it along his thick length. *He's fucking huge.* My chest heaves—a mixture of nervous excitement and the tingling in my clit—as I wrap my hand around him and feel how hard he is.

"Fuck, you feel good," he gutturally exhales from my attempt to stroke him through his pants. Letting me continue, he lifts his hips and inches his sweatpants over his them until every glorious inch of him flops out. I wrap my hand partially around him and slide it repeatedly from base to tip as I continue to ride his leg. His hips lift to meet my hand, and he groans before commanding, "Show me what a needy slut you are. Fist my cock as you make yourself come."

Liam runs his fingers along the neckline of my camisole, his touch erupting goosebumps in its wake. He grips the fabric and pulls it down my body until my breasts spill over the top. Palming my breast, he kneads it before squeezing it in his fist. The tightness of his grip teeters between pleasure and pain, and the tension building at my core explodes. My back arches, and a breathy scream rattles from me as my clear, slick release soaks through my panties and saturates his pants.

"Oh fuck, sweetheart," Liam excitedly exhales with an almost laugh as I come down from my high. "For that surprise, I'll forgo you thanking me, but you will be strongly reminded if you forget again."

Liam fists the thin strap of my panties running over my hip with both hands and tugs until it snaps. He pulls at the other hip of my now-ruined panties until they are nothing more than a tattered piece of fabric in his fist. After haphazardly tossing them to the floor, he grips his shirt at the nape of his neck and pulls it over his head. He throws it toward my discarded panties and groans, "Had I known you were going to squirt all over me, I would've had you remove your panties, sweetheart. Be a good girl and come again, so I can watch that sweet pussy spray over my lap."

With labored breaths, I struggle to keep the pace Liam is demanding. His hand slaps my ass, the burn of his palm immediately replaced with the tinge of pain from him fisting the cheek. Using the tight grip, he roughly guides my movement as his lips wrap around my nipple.

He sucks it. Hard. His cheeks hollow as he continues to draw the tight bud deeper into his mouth until it's swollen and tender. He swirls his tongue around it, and my back arches once more from the pained pleasure. After grazing his teeth along the sensitive flesh, he releases me from his mouth and pinches it between his fingers. A feral moan rumbles from me when he rolls my already bruising nipple in his tight hold.

"So fucking receptive to my pain," he whispers. My clit throbs, and the pressure of my intense release is nearly unbearable. Squeezing my nipple harder, he pulls at it as his rough palm lands against my ass again, growling, "Is it going to make you come all over me?"

"Yes!" I scream the answer, my clit pulsating as my release splatters all over his lap. Struggling to breathe, I quickly pant, "Thank you."

Palming my ass with both hands, Liam pulls me into him, and his throbbing cock brushes against my already tender clit. He abruptly stands and quickly drops us both to the couch. Sliding his body down mine, he presses his hand between my thighs and plunges two fingers into me with such force that my toes curl.

Wrapping his hand around my throat, he thrusts his fingers and curls them against my walls. "A few more like that and you'll be ready for my cock."

CHAPTER TWENTY-FOUR

LIAM

Tightening my grip around Sasha's throat, I squeeze just hard enough to restrict her blood flow. *I want her to really let go.* Driving my fingers into her warm, wet cunt, I curl them against her G-spot. I quickly work at a punishing pace, jackhammering into her and demanding that she give me the messy release I want.

"Li...Liam..." she pants my name as every muscle in her body tightens. She clenches around my demanding, thrusting fingers, but I don't stop. I pump into her until her tight cunt spasms. After pulling from her, I strum my arousal-coated fingers over her clit and watch her slick, watery release erupt over my hand and her thighs. Her chest heaving, she struggles to catch her breath, but she forces out, "Thank you."

"Mmmmm..." I lightly slap my hand against her pussy, causing droplets of the wetness covering her to splatter over my hand. "You are fucking welcome. I could watch you come all fucking night."

I can't fucking get enough.

Plunging my fingers back into her, I grind them against her walls. She whimpers and cries as I both pleasure her and leave a painful trail of bites along her thigh. She tenses when I reach the scars—clearly left by Isaac—on her upper thigh. "Hurt. Not harm. I'll teach you how fucking good my pain can feel," I promise, peppering soft, wet kisses over every crude line.

Rubbing my thumb over her clit and curling my fingers inside her, I sink my teeth into her skin and suck her meaty upper thigh into my mouth. A pained mewl falls from her trembling lower lip, and I release the now-bruising flesh. "You'll learn to give yourself over to the torment of my pain." Pressing my lips to the deep purple mark, I leave a soft kiss. "Because this gorgeous fucking body is my thank you for the gift of your submission."

Staring at the marks left on her, I pick up my speed until I'm thrusting into her rapidly. I fuck her with my hand until I've pulled three more orgasms from her, and the creamy skin of her thighs tells the story of how I claimed her as my submissive.

I rub my fingers over her mound, spreading her glistening slick over her skin. We're both covered in her, and she's lying—*fully fucking satiated*—in a puddle on my couch. Lifting my hand, I give her pussy another firm slap. She moans with pleasure, and I can't help the delighted smile that spreads across my face. "Such a good fucking student," I groan, lifting my fingers covered in her to my mouth. Licking from my palm to my fingertips, I relish in her taste as I settle between her thighs.

As much as I would enjoy marking every last inch of her with my mouth as she spends the night coming around my fingers, I can't deny the need to sink my cock, which is tenting my sweatpants, into her. I fist her hips and yank her arse through the puddle beneath her until she's teetering on the edge of the couch. Her legs fall wide, putting her on full display for me. *It's a fucking invitation.* I press the thick head of my cock to her dripping entrance, but she's so fucking tight that it feels like I'm trying to push into a cock ring a size—or two—too small.

"You're going to take me, and I will not be gentle," I insist with my tip pressed into her wetness. "Cry if you need to. Let me know how good it hurts when I stretch out your tight little pussy." I hold her in place by gripping her hips and shove the entirety of me into her with a single thrust. "Fuuuuck," I grit through my clenched jaw as I quickly bury myself to the hilt, listening to a pained scream of bliss that rises from her lungs.

I slowly pull back a couple of inches from the tight vise of cunt, and her thighs tremble violently. "It's... it's too ...big," she pants her complaint as I slide back into her.

"It's not too big, sweetheart. Every inch of me is inside you." I take her hands, pull them to where our bodies meet, and rub them through the short tuft of hair surrounding my base. Placing her hands on her slippery thighs, I help her to pull the tight hole wider. Providing a little reprieve for us both, I command, "You can take me. Hold yourself open while I fuck you."

True to my word, I'm not gentle. *Not that I could be if I tried.* Every brutal thrust of my hips is fueled with unbridled carnal desire. *I fucking need her.* I slam into her, our skin clapping as my balls slap her arse from the savage way I claim her. She cries and moans through my thrusts, each bringing her quickly toward another release.

"You feel so fucking good," I grunt. *Too fucking good.*

Sasha's fingernails dig into the skin beside her pussy, and she struggles to maintain her hold when her thighs begin to shake uncontrollably. "I'm going to come again," she breathlessly cries.

Me fucking too, sweetheart.

"Soak us with your sweet fucking release," I demand, adding my thumb to her clit to push her over the edge. Her back arches as she writhes against the couch, screaming my name as she sprays over us both.

Pulling out, I vigorously fist my cock. "Fuuuuuuck!" I groan, painting my release over her glistening mound. My chest heaves—struggling to slow my loud, heavy breaths—as I watch our cum mix and drip down her swollen lips.

Sasha releases the tight hold on her thighs, revealing the bloody half-moons where her nails pressed through her flesh. When I melt into the couch beside her, she breathlessly exhales, "Thank you, Sir."

CHAPTER TWENTY-FIVE
SASHA

Sir?

The word spilled from my lips without a passing thought. *It's what he is.* While I have the option to walk away and end this arrangement at any point in time—*something my prior Doms would have never stood for*—he requested full control of me as his student.

Complete power.

24/7 governance.

My Sir.

Believing in his expertise, I followed my gut and trusted him enough to offer him my whole agency. The reservations I had are slowly subsiding—but definitely not entirely dissipating—with every day I spend getting to know him.

"I tend to prefer Master, but I do like the way 'Sir' trembles from those pouty lips of yours." Liam slips his hands beneath me and pulls my exhausted body into his. He rests my face against his bare chest and tucks my hair behind my ear. Sweeping his arm underneath my thighs, he cradles me as he rises to his feet. "It will be my honor to be your Sir."

He carries me across the apartment, and his words play on repeat in my euphoria-muddled thoughts. *It will be my honor.* Not his will. Not his command. His talk about dominance and submission isn't bullshit. He isn't taking or demanding my submission; he wants me to give it to him.

Cradled in his arms, Liam carries me down the hallway and into my ensuite. He lowers me to my feet, keeping a strong arm wrapped around my waist to hold me tightly to him as he turns the knob for the shower.

"What are you doing?" I utter, confused by his softness.

Liam tests the water with his hand. Confident it has warmed sufficiently, he walks us both under the stream. He pulls my back to his chest and continues to hold me snugly against him as he fills his hand with pumps of my body wash. Rubbing the rosewater-and-jasmine-scented suds over my stomach and down my thighs, a coy smile pulls at his lips when he finally answers, "You made quite the mess of us both, sweetheart. I'm cleaning us up."

"Why?" I blurt, my tone inadvertently rude. It's not that I don't appreciate his gesture, but it's a far cry from how I've been treated in the past. I've never had a man tend to the cuts and abrasions they left behind, let alone the cum they—*and sometimes their friends*—splattered over me.

Unfazed by what sounds like ungratefulness, Liam's hand dips between my thighs, and he tenderly rubs his palm over the suds-covered bites and bruises he left on them. "It angers me beyond words that you even need to ask me that," he gruffly whispers, pressing his warm lips to the wet skin of my shoulder. "I might fuck you like I don't care about you, but I have the utmost respect for you and your submission. Tending to you afterward is my way of making sure you know that."

Baffled by his response and uncertain how to respond, I stay silent as he continues to wash away all the evidence of both our releases. When we're both clean, he turns me in his hold and tips my face up toward his. "I will not be satisfied with our training until you learn to accept nothing less from your next Dom than the respect and adoration that I provide you," he promises, his gaze unwavering.

Turning off the water, he grabs a soft terry towel and wraps it around me before grabbing one for himself. "I can do that myself," I mutter when he begins drying me.

"I know you can, sweetheart, but you shouldn't *have* to," he whispers, running the towel down my legs. Clean and dry, Liam leads me to my bed, tosses back the covers, and gestures for me to climb between the sheets. He pulls the comforter over me and tenderly runs the back of his hand along my cheek. "You did very well tonight. Get some rest, Sasha."

His hand slowly drags from my face, and I immediately miss his touch. He turns on his heel to leave me, and I grasp for his hand. "Sir?" I murmur. "Will you stay with me?"

"Stay?" Liam repeats the word, his voice ticking up as he turns back to face me. I look up to find his brows slightly furrowed. Immediately feeling like I crossed a boundary I shouldn't have, I let his hand slide from mine. I roll away from him and try to bury my face in the pillow, desperately trying to hide my embarrassment as I pull the covers up to my chin. Liam expels a slow, heavy sigh, alerting me that he is still beside my bed.

"Scoot over," Liam gives the gentle demand.

Great... A pity cuddle.

Without turning to face him, I mutter, "You don't have to."

"Sasha, I dislike having to repeat myself and definitely do not appreciate your overt violation of your rule about looking at me when you speak." He places his hand on my hip and gives it a firm squeeze. "Unless you want to be corrected for both transgressions, I suggest you scoot your gorgeous arse over."

I slide across the bed to the adjacent pillow to make room for Liam. The mattress dips, and he climbs in with me. "I know tonight was a lot for you, so I will stay until you fall asleep." Liam wraps his arms around me, and he pulls me into the warmth of his body. His breath blows over the crook of my neck as he holds me in his embrace. Relishing in the comfort and safety of his body wrapped around me, it only takes moments for my exhaustion from tonight to consume me. As I drift off to sleep, I barely register the words he speaks softly against my ear. "But I don't want you to get the wrong idea. You need to remember what this is. You're my student, and I'm your teacher."

CHAPTER TWENTY-SIX
LIAM

You're my student, and I'm your teacher.

My words are hurtful—*I know they are*—but they're as much for me as they are for her.

Never again...

It's why I have rules for myself: separate bedrooms, contracts, and not letting any woman serve as my submissive for more than a few months. Each has a purpose. They all maintain the firm line I draw between an arrangement and a relationship. I lie and tell myself it's so the women I temporarily bring into my life don't become too attached. So they don't get hurt when our time together comes to an end.

Yet, when Sasha asked me to climb into bed with her... Her soft request rang through my ears like a pained plea, and I couldn't stop myself.

Just like I can't seem to stop myself from doing a lot of things when it comes to her.

When I broke my own rules and slid into bed with Sasha, one thing became abundantly clear. *It's bullshit.* The only person I'm trying to ensure doesn't get hurt is me.

With her curvaceous arse nestled against my hips and her pert tits tucked under my arms, Sasha's body tucks perfectly against mine. *Too perfectly.* This is what I have been trying to avoid since Ella left. Holding her against me and listening to the sounds of her slumbered breaths, I can't deny how much I like this.

Or how much I like her... And how utterly absurd that notion is. I have only known Sasha for a few days.

Trying not to rouse her, I carefully pull my arm from beneath her and climb out of the bed. I let myself out and pull the door shut as I make my way across the hall. It's a futile attempt to put distance between us because all I smell when I slide between my own sheets is the sweet scent of jasmine.

I need a distraction.

It's late as hell, but I grab my cell phone from the nightstand and text my brothers.

> The lot of you have been awfully quiet.

DECLAN

> It's been quiet.

Ivan has been upholding his side of
the deal

I'll be back at the club in the morning.

Is everything taken care of for Sasha's
security.

Even my fucking distraction revolves around her.

RORY

Yes. Two guys will be at your place
before you leave in the morning.

TRISTAN

How are things with Sasha?

Good.

Too fucking good.

TRISTAN

I meant, how's she doing after
everything

Apparently, the bigger question is, how
are you doing?

This is the opposite of a distraction.

I'm fine.

DECLAN

That's almost as believable as when
Quinn says it.

I don't want to talk about it.

DECLAN

Exactly like fucking Quinn.

> If you don't want to talk, then just listen for a second.

> Take it from someone who speaks from experience…

> It's okay to care about her.

So much for my brothers taking my mind off everything. Silencing my phone, I toss it back onto the nightstand, angrily fluff my pillow, and bury it between my shoulder and the mattress. Rooting the side of my face against it, I will myself to sleep.

At least then, I won't be thinking about her.

CHAPTER TWENTY-SEVEN
SASHA

The sun blaring through the floor-to-ceiling windows forces me awake. With my eyes half closed as I adjust to the brightness, I feel the bed beside me for Liam. He was true to his word. I find the other side of the bed vacant and the sheets cold, except for a small black box and matching envelope atop the pillow.

Pushing myself from the mattress, I tuck the sheets under my arms to cover myself and grab the surprisingly heavy box he left behind. I lift the flap of the envelope and pull out the handwritten note.

Patrick and Harry (your security) are outside and will be ready to take you to lunch promptly at 11 a.m. My number and the club's have both been added to your phone.

Today's rules:
-Wear a dress.

-You answer when I call and follow my instructions without fail
-The contents of the box go wherever you do

Good girls get rewarded for good behavior,

– Liam

Tearing at the satin black ribbon, I pull it from the box and hastily remove the lid. I haphazardly pull the tissue paper from the box and toss it onto the bed until I reveal what he has given me—a mini wand.

Wrapping my hand around the small yellow wand, I lift it from the box and push the button to turn it on. The loud buzz of the heavy vibrations echoes around the room, only muffling slightly when I press its head against my palm. *Though she is small, she is mighty.* This is equally as strong as the full-size versions I have used —or had used on me—in the past.

Bringing the wand everywhere I go, I spend my morning tidying Liam's already immaculate apartment. Quickly running out of things to clean, I look through the cabinets to decide what to make for dinner. Surprised I've gone all morning without a word from Liam, I head into the bathroom to get ready for lunch.

Wanting to ensure I look good for his sisters-in-law, it took a little longer than expected to get ready. Glancing at my watch—*10:54 a.m.*—I quickly grab a purse from my closet to stow the wand and my phone. My phone rings from within the bag as I walk briskly to the door, not wanting to be late. When I pull it out, I find Liam's name on the screen and quickly swipe my thumb over it to answer as I reach the front door.

"Are you bringing your toy to lunch?" Liam asks before I have a chance to say a word.

Wrapping my hand around it inside my bag, I answer, "Yes. It's in my bag."

"Good girl," he praises. Barely taking a breath, he instructs, "Take it out of your bag, spit on it, and put it on your clit."

Seriously? **This** *is when he decides to call.*

Gathering saliva in my mouth, I drip it onto the wand as I lift my skirt. I pull my panties to the side, place it against my pussy and put my thumb on the power button before awaiting further instruction.

There's no way I won't be dripping down my legs with this thing...

"Don't worry about making a mess, sweetheart," Liam comforts as though he can read my thoughts. "You aren't coming. I want to listen to you bring yourself right to the edge. You better hurry up and turn it on, though. You wouldn't want to be late."

Pressing the button, the throbbing vibrations immediately rattle me to the core. "Fuck." The breathy grunt flies from me, quickly followed by a slew of uncontrollable moans. My chest heaves as my clit throbs against the flutters of the wand. I try to fight it, but it's so strong that it quickly has me hurtling toward the brink. I bite at my lower lip, and a pained whimper falls from my lips.

"Mmmm... That sound..." Liam purrs. "You're so close, aren't you, sweetheart?"

"Yes," I cry softly.

"How far can you go?" he taunts. "Can you give me another thirty seconds of those sweet fucking sounds you make?"

With trembling thighs, I respond, "Yes, Sir."

"Good girl," Liam croons. *I'd go another thirty minutes to hear him praise me again.* My knuckles grow white as I violently clench the wand in my fist, struggling against my need to come. Seconds tick by like hours, and he finally instructs, "Turn it off."

I've been denied more times than I can count, but not once have I had to deny myself. The urge to disobey him and provide the relief I need is overwhelmingly strong, but I force myself to follow his command. My clit is throbbing when I pull the wand from it. I turn it off and struggle to catch my breath. My heavy breaths echo down the phone, nearly drowning out Liam. "You're going to be late for lunch." His tone is cheeky and playful. "Talk to you soon, sweetheart."

The phone goes silent, and I pull it from my ear to find he has hung up. I note the time—*11:00 a.m.*—as a loud knock rattles the door before me. Shoving the wand and phone back into my purse, I quickly smooth down my skirt and open the door.

The tall, red-haired man on the other side of the threshold quickly takes in my labored breaths and what I can assume are my flushed cheeks and gruffly asks, "Are you okay, ma'am?"

"Fine," I respond. Embarrassed—*and wondering if he could hear me from the other side of the door the whole time*—but fine.

CHAPTER TWENTY-EIGHT

LIAM

Moments after hanging up the phone, I already want to call her back. *At least I don't need to wait too long.* Thinking about our next call, I can't fight the devilish smile spreading across my face.

"What the fuck?" I blurt, finding Conor standing behind me when I turn to rejoin my brothers in the lounge. Pushing past him, I gruffly ask, "Were you listening the whole fucking time?"

"Not the *whole* time," he emphatically draws out his answer. "I came to ask you a question about the time she said 'fuck.' You had her on speaker, and I'll be honest, I was too intrigued to walk away."

"Too intrigued to walk away from what?" Finn chimes from the bar when we loudly enter the lounge.

"Nothing," I huff.

"Did you seriously just deny that poor girl over the phone?" Conor asks, not taking my overt hint to drop the matter.

"You listened to the whole call," I snark. "Do you really need to ask that?"

"I'm over here trying to see if it's actually possible to cause one of these women to orgasm to death, and you're not letting her come on purpose? Hasn't she been through enough?" Conor snarkily jests.

"Because you're so fucking nosy, what"—I air quote—"she's been through, is why I am doing what I am." I take a seat at the bar, and Conor eagerly takes the seat beside me, clearly expecting me to elaborate on my prior statement. *Something I was not planning on doing.* "You're not going to let this go, are you?"

"Nope," Conor responds, with an exaggerated shake of his head.

"And fuck," Finn grabs a seat as well, "As a proud member of the How Many Times Can I Make Her Come Club, I'm also fucking intrigued."

Why couldn't my parents have given me sisters? Ones who would only be interested in whether she was emotionally okay...

"After what happened to her here, common fucking sense should make it pretty clear to all of you that I can't play with her as I would with pretty much anyone else. I'm hesitant to so much as break out a crop with her until I know for certain she trusts me," I explain.

"And edging her, of all things, is going to help her to trust you?" Conor scoffs.

"Yes," I answer matter-of-factly. "I was very clear before the wand was even switched on that she would not be coming, and I upheld my word. She chose to obey me and is expecting to be rewarded for doing so, which she will be."

Eventually.

"It's small steps to prove to her that I'll do what I promise. I want her to be comfortable with me, so she knows when she calls 'red' that I'll stop for her. Seriously, have neither of you ever trained a sub before?" The two of them stare at me, and I suddenly feel like I'm teaching a beginner's class in dominance. Turning my attention to Finn, I rhetorically ask, "Didn't you *just* marry a girl with zero lifestyle experience?"

"I think we all know that Cat trained his arse," Conor laughs as he nudges Finn.

"The whole time that the lot of you gave me shit for giving up sex, I was spending hours every night sitting on the sidewalk with Cat. Talking all night, getting to know her and earning her trust," Finn shares. "So, I get what you're saying."

"Plus, Liam likes her," Tristan teases from a nearby seat.

"For fuck's sake," I snip.

"What?" Tristan shrugs. "You killed Isaac for her the night you met. More correctly, I watched you *enjoy* torturing a man for hours for her."

Feeling my face fill with anger just thinking about his name carved into her thigh, I snarl, "If any of you had seen what that piece of shit did to her, you would've fucking killed him, too."

"I know any of us would've beat him to death, but what you did... That was personal," Tristan presses.

Sometimes, I hate how well we all know each other.

I was going to beat the fucking piss out of him for what he did to Sasha. After spending a few short hours with her, thoughts of pummeling my fists into his face until one of us broke was no longer enough. He deserved to experience the death he nearly took her life with. *She* deserved to know that he left this world with the understanding that she was the reason I was denying him his final breath.

"Killing him wasn't enough, though, was it? Because you pushed to move her into your place two days later. And I'm going to assume if you're listening to her not come over the phone, it's because you've had the pleasure of enjoying it firsthand. So, you're clearly fucking her," Tristan continues with his musings. "I knew Layla was mine before the end of our first date. Finn fucking gave up strippers the minute he bumped into Catlin. None of us will judge you for admitting you might actually like her."

"It's not like that." I shake my head, continuing to deny —*mostly to myself*—what he's saying.

"That's the only rebuttal you have?" Tristan chuckles. "Very convincing."

"Let him alone," Declan gruffs, and I'm relieved to have one of my brothers on my side. My relief is short-lived when he continues, "It took me nearly two years to admit to myself that I still loved Quinn—"

"I don't love her," I interrupt, quickly realizing how defensive my brash statement sounds.

It's not a lie.

I don't love her.

I just can't stop fucking thinking about her... Wanting to take care of her... Worrying about her...

Fuck...

CHAPTER TWENTY-NINE
SASHA

The restaurant Layla chose is small and cozy, tucked away in a side street with a shabby-chic charm. Every mismatched chair is occupied, and the space buzzes with conversation. Spotting Layla at a table toward the back with a blonde, I make my way through the crowded space and take the empty seat beside her. Worried that I may miss Liam's call with how loud it is in here, I rudely place my phone face up on the table and mutter, "Sorry I'm late."

"No worries. We've only just got the table." She shakes her head and pulls me in for a hug. After introducing me to Catlin, Finn's wife, and informing me that Quinn, Declan's wife, couldn't make it, I get the details of the Evans family tree. *Not that I will remember all these names without faces.* Conversation flows between the three of us—like picking up with old friends—as we share an array of appetizers and wine.

Layla orders a second bottle of rosé for the three of us to share as Liam's name lights up on the screen of my phone. I snatch it from beside my plate and quickly answer, "Hello?"

Liam's gravelly voice carries through the phone. "I want to hear that desperate little whimper of you on the edge again."

"I'm still at lunch with your sisters-in-law," I inform him, trying to keep my tone conversational so as not to alert my new friends.

"Trust me, they'll all understand," he retorts, with a slight playfulness. "If you don't want the restaurant to watch, you have exactly two minutes to excuse yourself and find a restroom."

He can't be fucking serious.

"Which is it going to be, sweetheart? I'm waiting. And the clock is ticking."

Fuck...

"Um... I...." I stammer and gesture at the phone in my hand. "I'll be right back. I need to take this." Grabbing my purse, I make a beeline to the restrooms in the back corner of the restaurant. Once I've slipped inside, I lock the door and quickly check the two stalls to ensure I'm alone.

"Fifteen seconds," Liam warns as I scramble to pull the wand from my purse and lift my skirt. "And I want to watch this time. Prop the phone on the counter."

Doing as he asks, I click the button to accept the transition of our phone call to FaceTime. When I step back, I pause to check if I'm on the screen before turning on the wand and placing it between my thighs.

"You're such a good fucking girl. And such a dirty little slut, playing with your pussy in public for me," he praises. A shuttered moan rattles from me, and I'm unsure if it's from the heavy throbbing between my thighs or the way Liam speaks to me. "Is it being called a good girl or a dirty slut that elicits your whimper?"

"Yes," I pant, quickly losing control of my breathing. "I mean... both."

"My good little slut"—*oh, fuck...my pussy definitely likes that*— "looks fucking gorgeous with her skirt hiked around her waist and that perfect fucking pussy on display just for me."

The wand violently flutters against my clit, and I slap my hand over my mouth—in a futile attempt—to stifle the sounds of my pleasure. My palm muffles my throaty cries, but they are far from silenced as I quickly bring myself to the edge.

"So fucking close already," Liam whispers. "So fucking eager to come for me, aren't you?"

"Yes... Sir." My breathy reply carries the pain of a desperate plea, the ache of needing to come quickly growing unbearable.

"Not yet, sweetheart," Liam groans, shifting this weight and adjusting himself. "I want you to spend the afternoon knowing that my cock is fucking throbbing from the thought of having you come against my tongue and then again as I sink into that tight pussy of yours and use you like the good little toy you are."

"Please..." My thighs shake, and I rub the wand against my clit, bringing me to the cusp of releasing the tension building at my core. I bite my palm, hoping the pain distracts me long enough to ward off the impending orgasm from the aggressive toy pressed against me.

"That's enough," Liam commands, seeing how close I am to coming. I don't hesitate to listen and immediately switch off the wand. "I want you needy and dripping by the time I get home."

Mission fucking accomplished.

The hand dryer could blow against my clit, and I'd probably come right now.

"Go enjoy the rest of your afternoon." Liam smirks before ending the call. Walking toward the sinks, I drop my skirt down my thighs. I give both my hands and the wand a quick wash. Shoving it back into my purse, I take a quick glance at myself in the mirror.

Yup, totally looks like I just got fucked in here.

I take an extra couple of seconds to straighten my clothes before heading back to the table. When I take my seat, Layla leans toward me and loudly whispers, "Did you just get fucked in the bathroom?" A knowing giggle rattles from her, and a broad smile spreads across her face when my eyes blow wide. "No judgment. I've definitely been put in my place in quite a few restaurant bathrooms."

"H-how did you?" I softly stammer. "I... I mean, I... I didn't."

"Your face has that just-got-railed-bent-over-a-bathroom-sink look to it," she shares with a chuckle. "I didn't see Liam, though. Did he sneak out the back?"

"He was on the phone," I respond, suddenly feeling the flush on my cheeks grow a bit more heated. "It's a game... or a test ...today. He calls, and I have to—"

"Say no more"—Layla interrupts me with a wink—"but that's fucking hot." My admission fazes neither Layla nor Catlin. The conversation carries on as though edging yourself in the bathroom is completely normal. *Just another Tuesday.* The lunch crowd dwindles, and we are one of the few remaining tables by the time we finish our second bottle of wine.

"Liam asked us to take you shopping," Layla informs me as she takes care of the check.

I shake my head. "That's unnecessary. I have a full closet of things he already got for me."

"Technically, I got those for you." Layla laughs. "I won't force you to go or to buy more things, but that's because I'm pretty sure it'll be your backside that pays the price for not doing as he asked."

CHAPTER THIRTY
SASHA

"The man wants to spoil you, I suggest you let him and maybe bring home something to let him know how appreciative you are." Layla smirks, shaking a risqué, crotchless white negligée in my face. I snatch the hanger from her before Patrick, Harry, or the two other guys watching over us catch a glimpse of it.

Surrounded by lace and satin, I run my fingers over the expensive fabrics with a heavy, uncomfortable sigh. *I'm not used to being doted on.* Catlin lifts a delicate black lace bra from the nearby display and holds it up. "What do you think?"

"That's hot," I admit. "You should definitely get that."

"I meant for you." Catlin smiles and lowers her voice. "Finn would destroy this the first time I put it on." She finds a pair of tiny matching lace panties and passes both to me.

Layla grins. "See? We're already making progress."

The two of them load me up with more lingerie than any woman needs. That said, Liam is currently 1-0 with my panties, so I'm already down a pair. If they're going to be torn from me, this might not be enough.

"You aren't getting anything?" I ask Layla as the three of us make our way toward the fitting room.

"I'm not allowed," she answers frankly. "Tristan finds panties to be a hindrance and has forbidden me from wearing them. *Ever*."

"Oh... I guess I would understand that if you were buying the sensible panties Catlin is," I tease.

"I own sexy panties, too," Catlin quips, crossing her arms. "I like comfort, and I happen to be adventurous in other ways. Besides, thongs chafe when you're running through Central Park trying not to get railed on the running path."

All of us laugh—a comfortableness filling the space around us—and I realize that this Liam-prescribed shopping trip is about far more than getting me more clothes I don't need. It has been arranged to give me the opportunity to bond with Liam's family.

The next few hours pass in a blur of trying on lingerie, dresses, heels, and new running shoes for Catlin. All of us leave with enough bags that the men watching over us are forced to help carry things to the matching black Suburbans in the parking garage.

"This was actually not horrible," I admit, giving Catlin a hug goodbye. "I had fun getting to know both of you."

"The boys might not like it." Layla rubs her fingers together, referencing the gross amount of money we've spent. "But we should do this again soon."

"Definitely!" Catlin agrees. "We should make this a regular thing."

"We can break the news to them during family dinner this weekend," Layla chuckles.

"Family dinner?" My voice ticks up. "That's a real thing?"

"Every week," Layla smiles. "It generally happens at Quinn and Declan's place in New Rochelle since it's the biggest by far. Between the five brothers, Rory, the now four of us, three kids, and sometimes Jorge, we need all the space we can get."

"This weekend?" I repeat, suddenly nervous about meeting the rest of Liam's family.

"Don't stress." Catlin lightly grips my hand. "The boys will all fawn over you, Conor will make relentless jokes about wanting to sleep with you, and Liam will probably beat the snot out of him for it."

"It'll be a nice change from Finn or Declan fighting with him," Layla giggles.

The three of us say our goodbyes, and I slide into the back of my SUV. We have no more than pulled from the parking spot when my phone dings with a message from Liam.

> LIAM
>
> Did you have fun, sweetheart?
>
> I did.
>
> They are so wonderful and welcoming.
>
> Good.
>
> I just got home. See you shortly.

This close to rush hour, it takes forever to make our way across town to Liam's apartment. We finally reach our destination and park in the garage. Patrick opens my door and helps me from the backseat as Harry grabs my bags from the back. "I'll bring these up for you, ma'am."

"Thank you," I mutter, still very uncomfortable with the treatment I'm receiving. We ride the elevator in silence, and Harry follows behind me into the apartment with my many bags in tow.

"Did you leave anything at the store?" Liam teasingly scoffs when he sees Harry's full hands. "You can place them in her room, and she won't need you or Patrick for the rest of the evening," he tells Harry.

"Of course, sir." He nods, quickly disappearing down

the hallway. He returns moments later and silently lets himself out as Liam leads me toward the kitchen.

Liam leans against the counter and picks up his glass of whiskey. He takes a slow, savory sip and asks to hear more about my day. He listens attentively to every word, showing genuine interest in the mundane details of my day.

"Are you hungry?" he asks when I finish.

I shake my head. "Not really."

Liam finishes his drink places it in the sink, and rounds the island to the barstool I'm sitting on. "I'm glad you enjoyed your day." He smiles, parting my knees and sliding the back of his hand along my inner thigh. His fingers dust along my panties, and I bite my lip as his light touch quickly reminds me of how needy he has repeatedly left me today. Gripping my hips, he pulls me from the stool to my feet and tucks my hair behind my ear. "I enjoy seeing a smile on that stunning face of yours."

CHAPTER THIRTY-ONE

LIAM

"You did such a good job following my rules today, sweetheart," I croon, softly dragging my knuckles along Sasha's jaw. Her skin warms under my tender touch, and her eyes fill with lust as I stare down at her with both pride and adoration. *She follows my commands and rules so fucking well.* I slip my fingers under her cream, cashmere open-front cardigan, and my hands slide over the soft, bare skin of her shoulders as I slip it from them. The fabric slides down her arms, and I push it over each of her hands and let it fall to the floor.

With my lips pressed to her shoulder, I slowly gather the fabric of her loose dress into my fists. I pepper kisses along her collarbone and neck until her dress is bunched around her waist. "I believe I promised to reward you for good behavior," I whisper with my lips dusting against the shell of her ear. She lifts her arms as I pull the slate-gray dress up her torso and over her head. I drop it to the floor with her cardigan, leaving her before me in nothing but a matching black bra-and-panty set and a pair of stiletto booties.

And fuck, is it ever a sight.

I hoist her onto the countertop and can't help but snicker at the tiny squeak she exhales when her bare arse hits the cold marble. Sliding my hands over her hips and down her thighs, I part her knees to make room for me. I lower my face to her lace-covered pussy. She lets out a sweet, needy whimper as I lick over the sheer fabric with the flat of my tongue; the sound is like a fucking drug.

I need more.

Slipping my fingers beneath the lace of her panties, I pull them to the side and place a wet kiss against the plump lips of her pussy. My tongue slides through her slit with my second kiss, dragging along her smooth flesh as I relish in the taste of her. Moaning with delight, I groan into her, "Your cunt is sinfully fucking delicious."

Palming her ample tits as I kiss over them, I free them from the lacy cups of her bra. The tight peaks of her hardened nipples rub against my palms. Skimming my palms along her heaving breast, I pinch the tight pink buds and roll them between my fingers as I tug at them. Sasha's ever-responsive body reacts to every touch, leaning into me and pleading for more. "How does my good girl want to come?" My question is muffled against her heaving tits.

She looks down at me with uncertain eyes, and her breathy voice raises an octave. "Sir?"

"You're coming on my tongue," I clarify, pressing my finger into her and rubbing the pad of my thumb around her swollen clit. Curling my finger and slowly dragging it along her walls, I ask, "Do you want it with or without my fingers?"

Continuing to teasingly work my fingers in her pussy, I stare up at her as I await a response. Her answer doesn't come, though, and it leaves me wondering why she's so hesitant to answer such a simple question.

"You've earned this, sweetheart."—I cup her face with my free hand and still my finger—"Just as I'll correct misbehavior, I want to show you how much I appreciate when you give yourself over to me. Tell me how you want me to please you."

She hesitates, struggling to hold my stare. Her response is so timid that it's barely audible. "Fingers."

Resuming curling my finger, I hold her gaze as I kiss down her stomach. Between lingering wet kisses, I ask, "Fast and hard? Or slow and tender?"

"S...slow."

I'll happily take my time feasting on you.

"I expect to be soaked with you by the time I'm done," I softly command as I bury my face in her pussy. My tongue swirls around her hardened clit, and I savor both her taste and the sweet whimpers trembling over her lips as I take my time licking and sucking her toward her release. I press a second finger into her tight channel, and she groans with pleasure. I match her moan, my cock growing rigid with the anticipation of feeling her wrapped around me again.

"Show me how my good girl comes on my tongue," I urge between swipes of my tongue. "Then I can show you how my fuck toy comes on my cock."

Sasha's arches into my touch, silently asking for more. I apply more pressure with my fingers and tongue. Her labored cries grow louder, and she writhes against my face as she teeters on the edge. As much as I want to nip at her clit and firmly thrust into her to demand her release, I maintain my slow, steady pace.

Her clit throbs against my tongue, and she quivers around my fingers. My tongue glides through her slick pussy, and a soft, breathy scream rises from her lungs. Sasha's head falls back, and her delicious, watery release cascades down my chin. Placing a final kiss on her wet mound, I pull my glistening fingers from her.

Gripping the back of my arousal-dampened shirt, I pull it over my head and toss it to the floor. Sasha sits at the edge of the counter, her breaths heavy and labored, as I undo my pants. I shove them down my thighs, allowing my rigid cock to spring free.

"Thank you, Sir," she exhales on a ragged, satisfied moan.

Such a good fucking girl.

"This won't be as gentle." I grip both hips, dragging her from the counter and to her unsteady feet. Abruptly spinning her around, I bend her over the counter and drive the entirety of me into her with a growl. "But my dirty little fuck toy is going to love it."

CHAPTER THIRTY-TWO

SASHA

The slow, tender worshipping of Liam's tongue has me riding a euphoric high. Coursing with bliss, Liam drives into me, and a ragged moan billows from me as he stretches me to the brink with ease.

"I marked your thighs with my mouth," Liam reminds me of the bites and hickeys running along the uppermost parts of my legs. He slams his hips against my ass with a hard, deep thrust as his palm rubs my ass cheek, gravelly whispering, "Tonight I'm going to mark this perfect, round arse with my hand."

I involuntarily gulp, my body tightening as a sudden pang of fear shatters my euphoric state. Liam's fingers tangle in the hair at the nape of my neck, and he gently turns my head to the side. "You can do this," he assures me when I meet his gaze from the corner of my eye. *Hurt. Not. Harm.* Taking a deep breath, I expel my hesitation on an exhale. As I relax beneath him, Liam lets out a soft, satisfied, "Mmmm. Good girl."

He lightly slaps my ass cheek, and the crisp sting burns for a second. Rubbing over the area he struck, Liam thrusts the entirety of himself into me. He drives into me repeatedly, finding an eye-roll-inducing, steady, and enjoyable pace. Arching my back, I lift my hips from the counter and push backward to meet his pleasing thrusts.

A hand lands across my backside—slightly harder than the last—as Liam buries his cock in me. The pleasure of his thrust dulls the burn of his strike. "Does my good little toy like that?" he taunts, repeating the combination, and a tremulous groan rises from my lungs.

His hands on my skin don't hurt like it did with anyone else. This doesn't feel nefarious. There is so much pleasure mixed with every thwack. He wants me to enjoy this. *And I am.* His pain hurts, but it also feels good. *So fucking good.*

"Hands on the counter," Liam commands, his tender and reassuring tone growing darker and more demanding. "Breathe into the pain, sweetheart, because the next one won't be gentle."

His hand continues to rub over my ass, warming my flesh before striking it hard enough that I stifle back a moan. He swats at my other cheek, and a tiny, uncontrollable groan rattles from my lungs.

"Your sweet fucking pussy grows wetter with every mark I leave on you," Liam groans, my arousal audible with every drive of his cock. "It's practically begging me to spank your sweet arse until you're unable to sit."

"Please, Sir." The cracked words erupt from me, surprising even myself. As much as I want to please him, I'm asking this for me. For the first time, hearing those words doesn't sound like a threat. Nothing Liam says sounds like a threat. Instead, they sound like an enjoyable promise. *An honor.*

Rubbing over my warm skin with one hand and tightening his hold on my locks with the other, his tone is dark—yet pleased—as he instructs, "More, your safeword, and Sir. Those are the only three words I want to hear pass over those pretty pink lips." He doesn't give me a chance to respond. The crack of his palm connecting with my ass echoes around the room as tears well in my eyes. He rubs his hand over the tender skin as he slides himself in and out of me, quickly alleviating the pain.

My heart races and my nipples slip along the icy countertop with every ragged breath. I wait for him to do it again. *I need it.* Something in me demands to see how much I can enjoy. "More..." Without hesitation, his hand lands on my ass again. Liam gives me exactly what I'm asking for as I beg for more. He fucks and spanks me until the entirety of my ass is red, arousal streams down my thighs, and I'm quivering around him as the pleasure swelling at my core is ready to explode. "More," I tearfully plead.

Increasing the pace of his thrusts, Liam glides his hand over the hot skin of my ass. He takes me hard, demanding my orgasm. A demand that I can't ignore. I yelp when his hand connects with my tender skin, and it sets off the explosion within me. Every muscle in my body trembles, and I cry out my release as cathartic tears cascade down my face. "Thank you, Sir," I sob.

Liam pulls from me, quickly flips me onto my back and lays me against the counter. "Let it out, sweetheart," he tenderly lulls, driving back into me to the hilt. Liam bends his body over mine and fucks me with deep strokes. Taking me hard and fast, working himself quickly toward his own release, he wraps my quivering legs around his waist. Every demanding stroke also quickly pulls another release from me. He stares down at me, watching fat tears trickle down my face as he slides his thick length into me. Sloppily kissing my neck, Liam groans through his thrusts, "Let it all go as you come around my cock."

His cock grows more rigid, grinding against my walls and pushing me over the edge. My mouth falls wide, and a near-silent scream flies out of me as I clench around Liam. His hips sputter and he pulls out, spilling over me with a guttural groan rattling in his chest.

Burying himself back inside me, he pulls me from the counter and into his arms. "You did so good," he praises, carrying me to the couch. He sinks into the soft leather with me straddling him as he grows soft inside me. Cupping my face with both hands, his thumbs tenderly brush over my cheeks to wipe away my tears. He doesn't admonish my tears or my feelings. Instead, he comforts and continues to praise me until my tears have all dried up. "I'm so fucking proud of you."

I lean forward slightly to press my lips to his, only to find myself denied again. He guides my head toward his shoulder and strokes my hair. Dusting his fingers along my spine as he holds me snugly against him, he painfully confesses, "I can't give that to you, Sasha."

CHAPTER THIRTY-THREE
LIAM

I can't...

I've already broken every fucking rule I have with her. *For her.* Tasting her lips will fucking ruin me, and I know it. She's already fucking ruining me. I keep denying what we both already know.

She has ruined me.

Kissing her will be my final straw, and I'll never be able to let her go.

Fuck, I don't know if I'll be able to already.

Sasha presses her soft, supple lips to the side of my neck, leaving a firm, wet kiss. Her lips and tongue drag along my skin, and she places another. I exhale a breathy groan and roughly palm her tender arse as she continues a slow trail of kisses up to my jaw.

"Can't?" Her sass-laced question vibrates against my skin and rattles me to my core. I should shove her off my lap, force her to stop. I want to, but not nearly as much as I need to feel her lips on my skin. *On my lips.* She sucks lightly at the skin above my rapidly increasing pulse, and my body betrays me, answering her question when my semi-hard cock twitches inside her.

She licks along the underside of my scruff-covered jaw, and I drag my tongue along my needy lower lip. Trying desperately not to lose what little control I still have over myself, I dig my fingertips into the red flesh of her arse. She laces her fingers in my hair and demands my gaze as she fights against my tight hold and swirls her hips over my now-rigid cock. *Fuck, everything about her feels so fucking good.* Further taking control and tugging lightly at my hair, she gruffly asks, "Or won't?"

Riding me and pulling my head back, Sasha dusts her soft lips against mine, and all I can think about is giving her exactly what she's asking for. *What she's demanding.* Her warm breath feathers over my lips as she repeatedly slides her slick cunt over my length. "Tell me you don't want to kiss me," she groans, and arches her back, burying me deeper in her. Pressing her lips against mine, she mutters, "Tell me you don't want to and I'll stop."

I'm far from a switch, but at this moment, I don't have an ounce of fight in me. I can't bring myself to correct her. *I don't fucking want to.* We both know I'll never fucking admit this on my own.

Dimpling my fingers into the soft skin of her arse, I delay my reply and rock into her. Her hips swirl, and I can't stifle my moan. My resolve dwindling, I fist her hair, and she winces when I roughly pull her lips from mine. Her eyes sadden as mine fall to her quivering lower lip. I tighten my hold on her locks, and her mouth gapes as she expels a pained breath.

"Fuck it," I snarl, yanking her mouth back to mine and giving in to what I've been denying myself since the moment I met her. Our lips crash against each other's, and I plunge my tongue into her mouth. *And I'm fucked.* With my tongue caressing hers, I claim her mouth. She matches my need, and we kiss until we are both well-beyond breathless, every swipe of our tongues fraying the thread of emotional detachment I was trying to keep between us.

Using my hold on her locks, I break our embrace. "We won't be able to go back from this, *mo mhuirnín*. You won't just be my student." With her chest heaving, she rides my cock and stares back at me with a longing need. *A need that won't be satisfied just by my cock either.* With my lips on hers, our lips vibrate when I tell her, "You'll be *my* submissive. You'll be *mine*, Sasha."

I don't need her to respond to know what she wants. *It's the same thing I want.* I've spent less time with her than any woman who has ever granted me their submission. Yet, I've never been so fucking sure about anything in my life.

Cupping her face and pulling her back into me, I groan into her mouth, "You'll be *mine*." My hands slide from her face and roam over the soft skin of her back as she rides me. Guiding her over my length, I kiss along her neck and chest before reclaiming her mouth. She whimpers into my mouth as her tight pussy quivers around my cock.

"Tell me who you belong to as you come all over me," I breathlessly demand through our kiss. I groan as she works us both to the edge and grit, "Tell me and I'll mark your sweet cunt as mine."

Her nails dig into my shoulders as she hurdles toward her release. "I'm yours." Her breathy words blow against my face as her lips drag along my cheek. "All yours, Sir."

Gripping her shoulders, I thrust into her from below. She presses her lips back to mine, and I claim her mouth, swallowing her moans as she comes undone for me. Her tight pussy pulsing around my cock is my undoing. "Mine," I grunt as I spill into her.

She lifts her arse to slide off my cock, and I grip her hips. "You aren't going anywhere, *mo mhuirnín*. You're going to sit on my cock and let me enjoy those soft, pink lips of yours until I grow hard again." I pull her back over my length. "And when I'm fucking ready, I'm going to bend over this couch and fuck you like you belong to me."

CHAPTER THIRTY-FOUR
SASHA

With swollen lips, a sore pussy, and a very tender ass, Liam carries me down the hall and into his room. He walks into the attached bathroom and sits us both on the edge of the tub. It's massive compared to the one in my room. Turning it on, he sweeps the hair from my face and confesses, "You're a mess, *mo mhuirnín*. Covered in our cum with trails of mascara staining your cheeks. A mess, but a beautiful fucking mess."

He tests the temperature of the water with his hand. Content with it, he pours salts from a small container on the edge of the tub, and they dissolve quickly in the steamy water. "This will also help with the soreness," he shares, swinging his legs over the tub's side and lowering us both into the hot water.

He's not wrong.

The water burns my sensitive skin as I adjust to it, but the heat of it soothes the sore handprints he left over my ass and thighs. Exhausted from hours of play and with the hot water relaxing me, I melt into Liam. I struggle to keep my eyes open as my head lolls on his shoulder.

"It's okay. I know I was hard on you. You must be tired." He places a kiss against my temple. "I've got you. I'll get you washed up and into bed."

My lids fluttering, I fade in and out of consciousness as Liam cleans the mess we made. He takes his time— gently and meticulously—washing every inch of my skin. The tub gurgles when he opens the drain, startling me.

"Stay with me for a moment," he urges, slipping from behind me. Water cascades down his body as he rises. Through heavy lids, I watch the remaining droplets trickle down his perfect physique. They roll over his rippled abs and down his sculpted thighs. *And fall from the thick head of his dangling cock.* Catching my gaze, he smirks. "I think you've had more than enough of my cock this evening."

With the soreness between my thighs, I don't try to argue. Even with all the foreplay, Liam is a lot to take. *Definitely more than my poor pussy is used to.*

Helping me from the tub, Liam takes equal care drying me as he did cleaning me. Once he's wrapped us both in towels, he ushers me into the bedroom. He pauses for the light, and I sleepily walk past the bed and toward the door. "Where are you going?" His question catches me off-guard, and I turn back to face him.

Confused, my answer mirrors his inflection. "To bed?"

"Again, where are you going?" He tosses back the white duvet on his bed and drops his towel to the floor. "Only students sleep in the other room. I think I was quite clear that you aren't my student anymore."

I stand rooted in place, so he crosses the room to me. His fingers dip into the top of my towel, and he pulls it off my body, causing it to ripple to the floor. "Maybe I wasn't clear," he gravelly whispers as he leans down to press his lips against mine. Kissing me passionately, he pulls my soft body against his hard muscles and claims my mouth until I'm breathless. After a few moments, he stops our kiss and arches a brow. "Do I need to explain it to you again, or are you going to get your sweet fucking ass into *our* bed?"

Sliding between the sheets with Liam, he turns off the light and brings me into his embrace. The dim lights of the city beneath his apartment cast into the room, and the outside world fades away as I snuggle against him. We lie in silence, and my eyes grow heavy. I listen to the soft sounds of our rhythmic breathing until sleep takes me.

When I awaken in the dark, I glance at the alarm clock. 1:27 *a.m.* Rolling over, I nuzzle Liam. He wraps his arm around me and whispers, "Go back to sleep."

Looking over his chest, I'm surprised to meet his gaze. My voice thick with sleep, I murmur, "Did I wake you?"

"No," he answers in a soft whisper. "I've been... watching you."

"Why?" I'm groggy, but I snuggle closer and find the comfortable spot in the crook of his shoulder.

Liam softly dusts my hair from my face and tucks it gently behind my ear as he confesses, "Because you're fucking magnificent..." His fingers dust over my skin, tracing the swell of my cheek and along my jaw. "And I don't know where you came from."

My eyes half closed and trying to stave off sleep, I mutter, "Long Island."

"Not quite what I meant." Liam presses his lips to the top of my forehead with a light chuckle. "I didn't see you coming."

Hooded with sleep, I hum, "You either, Sir."

"I didn't realize how good you would be for me." His fingers slide over my shoulder and glide along the length of my spine.

The heaviness of my lids demands I succumb to sleep, and my eyes fall shut. I shift my weight and curl my body into his, needing to be even closer to him, if at all possible. He wraps his arms around me a little tighter, giving me the comfort I'm seeking.

"Pulling you from that bench and breathing life into you, I never imagined..."

"Imagined what?" I run my heavy hand along the scruff of his jaw. Liam doesn't answer my question, and I'm too tired to press for an answer. My head lolling with the rise and fall of his chest, I listen to the sounds of our breathing again and find the world slowly slipping away as I drift toward sleep.

Liam exhales a light sigh as he presses his lips back to my forehead. They linger against my skin, and in this quiet moment, everything is just... perfect. He places another soft kiss and whispers so softly,. "That *you'd* be saving me."

CHAPTER THIRTY-FIVE

LIAM

"They're going to love you," I insist.

Sunday night Evans' family dinners are loud and chaotic. With the five of us, the women we've added to the mix, and Declan's ever-growing clan, the house is always filled with laughter, crass jokes, the occasionally spilled whiskey, and the ever-standard of someone getting the piss beat out of them. These days, that's generally Finn or Conor since neither can keep from flirting with women who aren't theirs.

"Conor and Finn might try to love you a little too much," I half jest as we make our way up the front steps. Sasha is hands-down Conor's type, and I fully expect him to salivate over her. "They are both harmless. And I'll fucking kill them if they aren't."

"*Uncail* Liam is here!" Fiona announces our arrival the moment I let myself through the front door. She barrels toward me and throws herself into my arms.

"How's my little nugget?" I adjust her in my embrace and tease, "I might have to just start calling you nugget. How old are you now? Twelve?"

"You're silly. You know I just turned six." She giggles. Leaning close, she whisper-shouts in my ear, "Who's your friend? She's pretty."

"She is pretty." I turn my gaze toward Sasha as I lower Fiona to her feet. "Her name is Sasha."

"Hi Sash—"

"Where's my peanut?" Finn shouts, letting himself through the glass door of the patio.

"Finnigan Evans," Quinn admonishes him from the entryway to the kitchen. "I swear to Christ, if you wake either of the twins, you're going to be the one spending the next hour getting them back to sleep."

I lead Sasha into the house and toward the delicious aroma coming from the kitchen, not once letting go of her vise grip on my hand. As expected, Conor's gaze rakes over Sasha's curves the moment she falls into his eye-line. Pushing from his perch on the kitchen counter, he crosses the room and exclaims, "*Go hálainn!*"

"Beautiful. Because you are," I whisper the translation against her ear. I watch her body language in hopes he doesn't elicit the same response I did at the hotel. She seems fine, but I feel compelled to make sure. "Are you okay?" She gives a slight smile and quick nod, confirming the word didn't trigger her.

"I knew you were fucking beautiful the first time we met, but you're fucking exquisite," he croons.

Sasha looks up at him, looking confused. "The first time? I don't think we've met before."

"Fuck. I beat the piss out of a fucking bloke for you and you don't even remember me?" he groans, playfully clutching his chest. His eyes hungrily roam down her body. "And here, I definitely remember all of you."

"For fuck's sake, Conor," I slug him on the shoulder. "Please tell me you aren't wanking off to that."

"I'm not into necro." He sounds disgusted. "But I'm pretty sure any mental images from this point forward are fair game."

"Jesus fucking Christ, Conor," Declan huffs from the island. "Could you find someone to whack off to that one of your brothers isn't sleeping with or married to? Would a subscription to Hustler help?"

"Probably not," Conor chirps. "I'll probably just imagine Ms. March buried between your wife's sweet thighs."

Declan looks at me and snarls, "I'm gonna fucking kill him."

"You aren't going to kill him," Quinn tenderly pats his cheek. "At least not until after dinner. I've been cooking for the past three hours, and it's not going to waste because the lot of you have to scrub blood from my kitchen floor."

"Because you asked so nicely, *mo chéadsearc*." Declan drags Quinn between his thighs and places a kiss against her lips. When he manages to pull himself away from her, I introduce them to Sasha.

"I'm sorry I missed out on lunch and shopping the other day," Quinn apologizes. "Little Rory wasn't feeling well, and I didn't want to leave him with a sitter. But short of this one"—she slaps Declan's chest—"tying me down to knock me up again, I will be there next time."

Rory walks inside from the patio, and I introduce him to Sasha, "And this is Big Rory." Her eyes dart between Rory, Quinn, and Declan as an inquisitive expression takes hold of her. I chuckle and answer the question I know is looming in her thoughts. "No. Rory was Quinn's security. He's not the twin's father."

"He better fucking not be," Declan hisses, half joking.

"Apparently, when you let the Bratva unload a clip into you and nearly die to protect someone, they name a baby after you." Rory smirks with a shrug. "And no offense, but I wouldn't be stupid enough to put my dick anywhere near Quinn."

"No offense taken." Quinn winks, gesturing for us all to make our way to the dining room. "I know I'm not your type."

Glasses clink, and we all dig into dinner; the table clatters with silverware, and the conversation grows loud and boisterous. The banter and jokes are loud and occasionally off-the-cuff, but Sasha slots in like a piece of the puzzle that's been missing. She jokes with my brothers and laughs with my sisters, and I find myself constantly staring at a smile I have seen far too little of in the time we've been together.

My family is a lot. And while they might've been too much for other women—like Ella—they seem to be absolutely perfect for Sasha.

After dinner, Sasha slips from the table with Layla and Catlin. I rest my elbows on the island and stare out the window to where the three of them sit on the patio as I roll my near-empty glass of whiskey against the white countertop. Catching my stare, Quinn squeezes my shoulder. "She's good for you."

Glancing up at her, I give a smile and nod in agreement.

Quinn leans against the counter beside me and rests her head on my shoulder. "I'm serious, Li. I've known you almost my whole life, and I've never seen you look at anyone the way you look at her," She shares, keeping her voice low.

Sasha turns toward the window and catches me watching her. A sheepish grin spreads across her face, and her naturally rosy cheeks redden. Watching her reaction, I can't help but smile back at her.

"And then there's that." Quinn playfully pinches my cheek. "I've never seen you this fucking happy."

CHAPTER THIRTY-SIX
SASHA

Curled into the corner of the couch, I read Jane Eyre for probably the fiftieth time in my life. My phone buzzes against my thigh, and I lift it to find a message from Liam, who should be returning from the club any time now.

LIAM

I left a present for you in the playroom.

The playroom? I chuckle to myself. Days after moving my things into Liam's room, he began renovations. All the feminine touches and dusty rose decor were replaced with black furniture and stainless-steel hooks as he filled the room with furniture more conducive to his tastes.

A St. Andrews Cross. A kneeling bench. A spanking bench.

And more impact toys than they probably have in the whole club.

The room and the items he has amply stocked it with have been used quite sparingly. For as rough as Liam likes to play, he has been very patient in taking his time with me. I might not be a stranger to being bound to a spanking bench, but after my last experience, he wants to be beyond certain that I am mentally prepared before asking that of me.

I place my book on the coffee table and bring my phone with me down the hall. Entering the playroom, I walk past the St. Andrews cross by the door and toward the large, upholstered charcoal daybed. I sit on it beside the large white box he left and run my fingers over the D-ring beside my knee and momentarily reminisce about the other night.

My legs cuffed to opposite sides of this oversized couch, and Liam teasing me for hours with the sting of a riding crop and velvety softness of his expertly skilled tongue.

The phone rings in my hand, quickly pulling me back from my daydream. I swipe my thumb over the screen to answer the call, and Liam instructs, "I want you ready and waiting for me when I get there."

As much as I know how he hates it when I brat, sometimes I can't help myself. "I don't know whether to be pleased or upset that going to the club makes you want to come home and play with me."

"Are you testing me, *mo mhuirnín?*" Liam snips. "Because I will damn sure test you in return."

"No, Sir," I quickly respond, knowing his threat isn't an idle one, and my ass will reap what I sow.

"Good, because I spent my night in the lounge," he shares. "I spent every miserable fucking minute staring into my glass of Jameson as I counted the seconds until I could come home to you. Grueling hours staving off my cock's excitement about the contents of that box and the *many* ways I'm going to fucking ruin you tonight."

My pussy flutters with as goosebumps prickle down my spine. Uncertain if I'm prepared for what this box contains, I hesitantly pull at the satin ribbon wrapped around it.

"You have ten minutes," Liam explains before disconnecting our call. I lift the lid and quickly examine the contents: lube, a moderately sized anal plug, a small key fob, black stockings, and a large leather paddle. Grabbing the lube, plug, and stockings, I head into the bathroom to ready myself for him.

Putting the icy cold plug in my mouth to warm it, I strip from my clothes and pull on the hosiery. I pull the plug from my mouth and wrap my hand around it—pleased it no longer feels frozen—as I pop open the lid on the lube. Slathering lube over the plug, I can't help but think that this will in no way prepare me to take his cock. *I actually don't know if I could accommodate him, even with extensive prep.*

I press the slick metal between my cheeks and rub the tapered head of the plug against my hole. Reaching between my legs, I lightly rub my clit. Liam owns my orgasms—and I wouldn't dare bring myself over the edge—but I need a little help to relax enough to ease the plug into my ass. As I teasingly work it inside of me, a groan rattles from me when it slips past my tight ring and it settles into place.

Liam's keys rattle in the door as I'm washing my hands. Turning off the water, I quickly dry them and toss the towel onto the vanity. Racing back into the playroom, I take a seat on the daybed seconds before Liam enters the room.

"Mmmmm," he groans, his eyes roaming between mine and my bare breasts. "You look fucking stunning. Let me see all of you."

Leaning back, I brace myself on my elbows. I spread my legs wide, granting him the view he wants of both my pussy and the plug buried in my backside. He slides his hand along my inner thigh and to the jewel nestled between my cheeks. Giving it a solid tap with his fingers, I moan as it momentarily pushes further into me. "Does that feel good?" He taps it again.

"Yes, Sir," I groan as he repeatedly jostles the base of the plug.

"I want you to focus on that pleasure," he commands, rolling me onto my stomach and pulling my ass into the air. Circling the couch, Liam's eyes roam hungrily over every inch of my skin as he strips to his black boxer briefs. Nearly naked, he steps between my feet and rubs both his hands over the bare cheeks of my ass.

"I'm not going easy on you tonight." He roughly palms my ass. "I'm going to paddle that sweet arse of yours until tears stream down your cheeks, your thighs are covered in need, and that tight little hole is clenched tightly around the plug."

Liam lifts the tiny key fob from beside me and holds down the button in the center. My thighs tighten, and I jolt when the first wave of vibrations tingle through my ass.

"Fuck..." I mutter.

CHAPTER THIRTY-SEVEN

SASHA

Liam rubs the smooth leather of the paddle over my ass cheeks as I adjust to the rhythmic pulsing of the plug buried between them. He snaps the paddle against my ass, peppering light swats across my backside. My skin warms at the repeated light taps, and I wistfully moan, yearning for more.

As though he can read my mind, Liam increases the intensity of the leather hitting my ass. The paddle hits my cheek with a slightly heavier thud, and a moan rattles in my chest. His fingers tangle in my hair, and he massages the nape of my neck and shoulders between swings. My senses heighten, and I am quickly overwhelmed with the pleasure and pain he's providing.

Teetering on the brink of my release, Liam tightens his hold of my hair, and the sweet pain radiates around my scalp. He lowers his face to mine, demanding my attention. "You do not have my permission to come," he sternly warns me. "You will not come. Do you understand me?"

"Yes, Sir," I breathlessly mutter. Clawing at the cushion beneath me, I fight desperately to quell the orgasm building at my core.

"Tell me you won't come," Liam commands, swinging the paddle.

It lands at the base of both my cheeks with a hard thud. A hot burn flashes across my skin, and I involuntarily clench my cheeks, tightening my already sensitive nerves around the vibrations I'm trying so desperately to ignore. "I won't come," I blurt so fast it sounds like a single word.

Liam drags his hand along the wetness of my entrance and darkly taunts, "Your pussy disagrees. You're fucking soaked."

"I won't come, Sir." I reaffirm my statement, trying to convince myself to believe it.

He slides his hands pleasingly along my spine as he bends over me. His hard cock presses against my ass as he lays his warm, bare chest against my back. He presses his lips just below my ear and gravelly whispers, "You're going to take ten more for me as we count them together. Each will be harder than the last."

"Ten." I inhale the word.

"Be a good fucking girl and I'll give that sweet pussy everything it wants." Retaking his place behind me, Liam presses the warm leather against my skin.

"One," I pant when the heat of the paddle flares over my skin. "Two... Three."

My pussy quivers as Liam pauses to rub over my tender skin. I suck in a deep breath, and tears trickle down my cheeks, but it's not only from the pain he's soothing. The need to come is unbearable, and it is taking every bit of my focus to keep it at bay.

"Four... Five..." I cry out. Every strike jostles the plug, demanding that I come. My nails dig into the cushion beneath me as though I'm trying to physically cling to the release I can't let go of yet. The paddle crashes against my upper thighs, and I grunt, "Six!"

"Fuck... This arse of yours is fucking gorgeous when it's marbled with my beautiful crimson marks. And it squeezes so hard around that little toy." Liam gingerly plays with the flared base of the plug. "I look forward to the day I get to bury my cock deep inside it. I can only imagine how beautifully you'll come as I stretch you to the brink."

My whole body begins to quiver. Every muscle in my body is fighting to betray me as Liam rests the paddle against my ass. I heave in another breath as he pulls it from me. "Seven!" I cry out my pain-fueled release as my cum rushes down my thighs.

"Did you just disobey me and fucking come?" Liam gruffs, but I can hear the tinge of pleasure in his voice. This whole scene was designed for me to fail. I was never supposed to make it to ten. Liam wanted to watch me break for him.

Gripping my arm and pulling me to my knees, Liam wraps his fingers around my throat and uses the grip to hold my back firmly to his chest. He runs his other hand across my chest, roughly palming at each of my rising breasts. Running his fingers down my stomach, he rubs firmly over my pussy and informs me, "Greedy sluts who come without permission get exactly what they deserve."

Liam drags me from the couch and places his hands on each of my shoulders. Applying gentle pressure, he nudges me toward the floor. "Kneel."

I hesitate, swallowing hard, with my body rigid. Trevor... *And the things his friends did as they stood over me... Isaac... The things he made me do to please him... Shawn... The rice... The fucking rice...*

"I dislike repeating myself," Liam barks, startling me. "Get on your fucking knees for me."

I drop to my knees, the thump of my fall echoing off the hardwood floor. *It won't be that bad. Just go somewhere else. You've done this plenty of times before.* Lowering my head, I watch Liam pull himself from his tight boxer briefs. His hand glides over his rock-hard length as he walks toward me, and I open my mouth wide to give him my apology.

"You don't get my cock yet. Not until I get to watch as you give yourself what you were so desperate for." He slips his fingers beneath my chin and closes my mouth. "Fill your dripping cunt with your fingers, and show me what you needed so badly that you had to disobey me."

I follow his instructions and press my middle and ring finger inside of me. *He's not like them, Sasha.* He takes a seat on the couch before me and languidly strokes his cock as I thrust my fingers into my pussy. *He'd never hurt you like them.* My knees grind against the hardwood floor as I ride my hand for him.

I stare at the floor and find it's bare beneath me. *It's not real, Sasha.* I groan in pain, feeling the tiny grains of rice Shawn spilled burrowing into my skin.

Stay here... With Liam.

My body sits on the floor before Liam, but my thoughts drift through my dark memories until I'm surrounded by the men who tried to ruin me. Each of them waiting to use me for their depravity.

CHAPTER THIRTY-EIGHT

LIAM

Sitting on the couch, I leisurely stroke my cock as Sasha's glistening fingers repeatedly disappear into her dripping cunt. Watching her pleasure herself is a heavenly fucking sight. *One I fucking can't get enough of.*

She fucks herself hard with her gaze fixated on the floor between her knees. "Eyes on me," I command. Her eyes don't pull from the spot they're focused. "I want to see your eyes as you make yourself come undone. Let me watch how sorry you are."

Ignoring my instruction, she silently slides over her hand. Her movements grow robotic and completely devoid of any enjoyment. *Something isn't right...* "Sasha." I try to hide my concern as I speak her name.

My calling her name goes unanswered, and I let my cock fall from my hand as I move toward her. When I slip my fingers under her chin, I lift her face from the floor and find tears streaming down her face. Her eyes are glassy. They stare in my direction, but she isn't looking at me. She's looking through me. Her fingers continue to work industriously between her legs, but she's... vacant.

This isn't subspace... This is something completely different.

"Sasha, sweetheart," I whisper, lightly swiping tears from her face as I desperately search the couch cushion for the plug remote. Finding it and fumbling for the button, I struggle to turn it off fast enough. *Fuck.* I drop to my knees with pained desperation. Slamming into the hardwood floor in front of her, I mutter, "Fuck, *mo mhuirnín.* What did they do to you?"

*What did **I** do to you?*

Reaching between her legs, I tenderly grasp her hand and pull it from inside her. I place a soft kiss against it and press it over the distressed thump of my heart. Gently, I scoop her into my arms and lift us both from the floor. Her heart is pounding so hard that it's reverberating against my arm as I hold her. "I don't know where you went," I whisper against the top of her head as I carry her down the hall to our room, "but I need you to know that you're safe with me, *mo mhuirnín.*"

I lay her on the bed, and she curls into a ball with her eyes closed. Her chest rises and falls with a sputtered, choppy motion, matching her heavy, ragged breaths. *Oh, sweetheart...* As much as I hate to leave her for even a second, I don't want her to wake up in the state she's in. I step into the bathroom just long enough to grab a wet washcloth and a towel to tend to her.

"I'm going to take care of you," I promise, wiping the trails of mascara from her cheeks. Softly, I lift her hand from the bed and clean the arousal from her fingers. I wash all evidence of our scene from her thighs, carefully extract the plug from her, and clean any remnants of lubricant from between her cheeks.

Haphazardly dropping everything on the floor beside the bed, I quickly grab two pairs of my sweatpants and a hoodie from the closet. I slip the far too-big sweatpants up her bare legs and pull the oversized hoodie over her head, then dress myself in the remaining pair of pants before climbing into bed with her. Resting against the headboard, I pull her listless body between my legs and rest her head against my chest. "I'm here, sweetheart," I mumble against her as I stroke her hair. "Whenever you're ready to come back, I'm here."

Sasha's heart rate slows, and her breathing becomes less erratic as she rests against me. I let her sleep against me and continue to comfort her as I wait for her to rouse.

The sun creeps over the city, and Sasha startles awake in my hold. "You're okay. I've got you." I whisper, tenderly tightening my embrace and pressing my lips to her forehead. "You scared me for a minute, *mo mhuirnín.*"

"I'm sorry," she murmurs.

"Hey"—I tip her face up to mine and shake my head—"You don't need to apologize, but I think we need to have a very serious talk about your safewords."

"I... I couldn't," she stammers.

Tucking her hair behind her ear, I respond, "*Always*. You can always use them. And I will adhere to them. Full stop."

"I was fine." Her voice is soft and timid. "And then I wasn't."

"There are nerves, and there is hesitation." I speak softly, wanting to impart that I'm not upset with her. "The second you have an inkling of feeling unsafe or thinking we need to stop, you *need* to use them. Because I don't ever want you to disappear on me like that again."

"Okay."

"Promise me," I insist.

Taking a deep breath, she lightly exhales, "I promise, Sir."

CHAPTER THIRTY-NINE

SASHA

"Now that we've settled that, are you going to tell me where you went?" Liam pushes, tightening his hold on me.

Burying my face against his chest, I grasp the front of the hoodie I'm swimming in for comfort before answering, "Some place bad…"

"Tell me because I don't ever want to be the reason you go there again."

I reach up to his jaw and pull his gaze to me as I slide my face from his chest. Meeting his eyes, I share, "You aren't the reason. I know beyond all doubt that you would never do anything to harm me. *Ever.* But when you forced me to my knees, I couldn't stop every last one of them from encroaching on my thoughts."

Wrapped in his warm embrace, I spend the morning telling Liam every abhorrent detail from my time spent with numerous wannabe Dominants before him. He comforts me—without judging me but vowing to kill each of them—as I provide the details of what I now know was my horrible mistreatment. *Abuse.*

"You should have told me, *mo mhuirnín*," Liam mutters. "I refuse to strap you to a bench and can't fathom gagging you because I know your history. The negativity you have associated with those practices has no place in our play for *our* safety. Had I known your history with kneeling, I would never have demanded that position of you."

"Dropping into the conversation that the last guy I was with would make me kneel on the concrete by the pool so his friends could use me like a urinal doesn't exactly slot into Tuesday night dinner conversation," I joke, trying to ease my discomfort.

"In this house, it does," Liam insists. "Tuesday night dinner, Saturday morning baths, or random Wednesday afternoon texts. There isn't a thing I haven't told you about my life, and I expect the same from you."

I would doubt his admission, but he spilled all of it to me as I moved into his room a couple of weeks ago and accidentally stumbled upon an engagement ring in the valet on the dresser. He told me all about Ella, how his life wasn't for her, and how he swore off caring for anyone like that again... Explaining why he was so hesitant to give in to us. When he was done, he shared so many sorted details of his life outside this apartment that I could single-handedly be the reason he—and his brothers—spend the rest of their lives waiting for the electric chair.

He's opened his closet and unpacked every one of his skeletons because he trusts me. "This thing between doesn't work if there are any secrets," Liam adds, further fueling the guilt I'm harboring for everything I'm still holding tight to my chest.

Liam slides from the bed as I find the courage to give him the last piece of me. I open my mouth and speak his name as he says, "I'm serious about eliminating all of them for you. I can't remove them from your thoughts, but I sure as fuck can remove them from this world."

"I know you would." With what he did to Isaac for me —*when he barely knew me*—I don't doubt him for a second. "But I don't need you to. They aren't part of my life anymore, and I don't need them to take up more space than they already have."

Climbing over me on the bed, Liam presses his lips to mine and pulls back with a smirk. "Dead men don't take up space, especially after they go through the crematorium. I'd let you watch. It's hot!"

"Oh, my God!" I playfully shriek, shoving him from me. "Did you just make a disgusting dad pun about burning one of my exes to ash?"

Rolling back on top of me, he presses me into the mattress with his weight. He leans down, stopping a breath from placing his lips on me. His playful eyes soften, replaced with adoration. "There are no limits to what I would do for you"—his confession blows over my lower lip—"to help heal you the way you've healed me."

Lifting my head from the mattress, I press my lips to his, and the two of us melt together. Liam presses his tongue between my lips and massages it against mine, his hand pulls my leg over his hip and settles him between my legs. Lacing my fingers through his hair, I break our kiss and stare up at him for a moment. "Sir..." I slide my palm along his stubble-covered cheek and confess, "You're going to make me fall in love with you."

"Good." A slow, broad smile spreads across his face as he hovers over me. "Because I'm fucking enamored with you, *mo mhuirnín*."

His lips crash back into mine, and I can feel every bit of his love as his tongue sweeps through my mouth. Running my hands down his back, I slip my fingers beneath the waistband of his sweatpants and push them over his firm ass.

"Are you sure," he asks against our kiss.

I lift my hips to rid myself of Liam's pants. Wriggling my leg free, I hook my knees over his hips as he rests the thick head of his cock against me. I wrap my legs around his waist and pull him against me, inching his long, thick length into me as I groan, "I've never been more sure of *anything*."

CHAPTER FORTY

SASHA

About THREE WEEKS LATER

"Can you pull over at the corner?" I ask Liam as we approach his building.

"What for, *mo mhuirnín*?" He squeezes my upper thigh as we approach the corner market.

"I just need to grab tomatoes for dinner."

His eyes dart back and forth across the busy street, and he shakes his head. "There's nowhere to park. The closest garage is nearly at our building. I'll call Harry. He and Patrick can run down here to grab them."

"Don't be silly." I place my hand over his and squeeze his hand. "Double park in front of the store and wait for me. I'll be in and out in two seconds."

"Two seconds," he gruffs, flipping on his hazard lights

and pulling to a stop beside the car parked in front of the store's entrance.

"Probably more like two minutes." I smirk and pull the handle to open my door. Slipping from the SUV, I promise, "I'll be fine." I jog across the sidewalk and briskly make my way through the grocery store to the tiny produce section at the back.

Lifting a tomato, I give it a light squeeze to make sure it's ripe but not too squishy before dropping it into the small plastic produce bag. I add two more to the bag, and as I reach for the fourth, I startle when a hand brushes my shoulder. Dropping the final tomato into my bag and tying a knot, I slowly turn around and tease, "I thought you were waiting in the car. Did you miss me that quickly?"

The hairs on the back of my neck stand on end when I'm met with a set of dark eyes instead of Liam's stormy blues. "We've *all* missed you, *malen'kaya printsessa*," he purrs. His eyes hungrily roam over my body, and a devilish smile ticks at the corners of his mouth. "But you apparently aren't so little anymore, are you?"

He runs his tattooed fingers along my jaw, and I pull from his unwanted touch. Swatting his hand away, my voice cracks when I snip, "I don't know you. Don't touch me."

"But I know you." He smirks, stepping toward me. I step backward to keep the distance between us, but my retreat is halted by the produce stand at my back. He leans forward against the stand, boxing me in between his arms.

My heart thumps in my ears as I begin to panic. I open my mouth to scream for help, but no sounds come. As much as I need Liam's help, this can't be how he finds out. He won't understand, and he'll never forgive me.

Fuck, I wouldn't forgive me.

I already hate myself for not telling him. It didn't matter when we met. When he took me on as a student, I told myself he didn't need to know. *Because he didn't.* We were temporary, and that part of my life —the one I had long before Viktor pushed me into this lifestyle—had no bearing on the years of training he wanted to correct. As I fell for him, I knew I had to tell him. But with all the time that passed, I couldn't. This insignificant secret wasn't nothing anymore. It was suddenly a massive fucking betrayal... A bomb that would implode the only relationship I've ever had with a genuinely good man.

A great fucking man...With a family I could have only dreamed of.

It's been years—*nearly six of them*—since I've seen a single person from that part of my life. The last thing I ever expected in a city of eight million people was a chance encounter to be the thing that outed me.

I've been in here far too long, and I fully expect Liam to come barreling into the store like the white knight he is within seconds. Taking a deep breath, I place my hand on the burly man's chest and shove him from me. "I said I don't know you."

"That may be so, but I definitely know you, Alexandra." He no more than finishes the name and my stomach flops. I swallow the bile rising in my throat and try desperately to hide my reaction as I walk from him. He calls after me, "I'll be sure to tell him you say hello."

Curiosity getting the better of me, I stop in my tracks and turn to face him to ask, "Who?"

"Your br—"

"Sasha?" Liam calls as he makes his way into the store. When I don't answer, his voice carries a tinge of worry. "*Mo mhuirnín?*" He spots me, his frantic gaze quickly softening when he finds me unharmed. *At least physically.*

"Are you okay?" he asks, wrapping his arm around my waist. Struggling to control my rapid breathing, I can only muster a nod. When I glance over my shoulder as Liam leads me toward the cashier, the man who cornered me isn't there. Nervously, I whip my head around and scour the store as we walk, but I don't see a trace of him.

"Y...yeah," I finally stammer, lying, as I squeeze Liam's hand on my hip. "I'm... I'm fine."

He pushes us past the short line and drops a twenty on the counter to more than pay for the bag of tomatoes I forgot I still had in my hand. Helping me into the Suburban parked in the middle of the street, he huffs, "We don't do that again." Liam shuts my door and quickly rounds the front of the SUV with his concerned eyes on locked on mine.

He knows...

CHAPTER FORTY-ONE

LIAM

Following her into the store felt overbearing until I spotted her. She was standing in the middle of the aisle, her face stark white, and she looked as though she had just seen a ghost. Even with the color returning to her face, her still-dilated pupils give away the fear she felt just moments ago.

I climb back behind the wheel, pull the door shut, and place my hand on her thigh. Giving it a tender squeeze, I ask again, "Are you sure you're okay?"

"Yeah," she answers softly, with a timid nod, as I pull into traffic. When I flip off the hazard lights, she blurts, "Just some guy…"

"Some guy?" I gruff.

"It was nothing." She shakes her head, dismissing the situation.

I tenderly run my hand along her thigh, gently retorting, "Your face says otherwise."

Sasha places her hand over mine and gives me a reassuring squeeze. "Really. It was nothing more than some jerk."

For weeks, she hasn't stepped foot out of my sight or from the apartment without Patrick or Harry hovering over her like a hawk. I don't know why I agreed to let her run into the store without me. *It was fucking foolish.* It only takes a second for someone to get to her. We're both lucky it was nothing more than some jerk who crossed a line and upset her. *Quinn. Catlin.* It could have easily been so much worse.

"Regardless," I huff. "We don't do that again. You have me and security for a reason."

Sasha doesn't argue. Instead, she is unusually quiet for the remainder of the short drive home. In the garage, I climb from the parked SUV and quickly round it to get to Sasha's door. She slides from her seat, and I pull her into me when her feet reach the concrete. "I'm not upset at you, *mo mhuirnín.* If I'm upset with anyone, it's me... For putting you in that situation." I hold her tightly while reassuring her.

Wriggling in my hold and rising onto her toes, she presses her lips to my jaw. Leaving a chaste kiss, she insists, "I'm fine."

"This time." I cup her face and stare down into her soft

brown eyes. "I'd never fucking forgive myself if anything happened to you."

"I know you wouldn't, Sir." She kisses me again.

Overwhelmed by the nagging guilt of what-if, I can't bring myself to pull my hands from her as we walk through the building and ride the elevator to our apartment. Stepping inside, I close and lock the door behind us before letting my hand fall from the small of her back. "I have half a mind to keep you locked in this apartment, where I know you'll always be safe."

"Don't you dare." She whips her head over her shoulder. "You promised."

"I'm pretty sure we didn't negotiate rules about locking you away to live your life as my hidden little fuck toy," I tease, pulling her into me again.

She shoves herself away from me, not the slightest bit amused by my less-than-grand gesture. "We agreed I could go and play at the club this weekend."

Since Sasha came into my life, I have spent very little time at the club. Any time I have spent there has either been during the day when we aren't open to the public or parked firmly in the lounge. Out of respect for Sasha, I haven't visited the dark hallways of the club. Our agreement forbids me from partaking, but I don't want to so much as observe without her present.

"I said we could *go* to the club," I sternly correct her. We have been arguing about this for the past week. Her attesting that she is ready and wants to attend with me, and me adamant that it's too soon to push her that hard. Or at least to commit to doing so. I won't agree to anything until I can assess her emotional well-being at the club to ensure we won't have a repeat of the kneeling incident the other week. "I have most definitely not agreed to take you into any of the exhibition rooms."

"Sir—"

"You put your trust in me to lead you and determine what is best for you," I interrupt her. Cupping her face, I place a warm kiss against her forehead before staring into the deep brown pools of her eyes. "I love you, *mo mhuirnín*, but I will not bend on this. Agreeing to go to the club this weekend is all that I will promise."

My phone buzzes in my pocket and stops me from rehashing this argument with her. Swiping over the screen, I shake my head when I read the message.

> TRISTAN
>
> Ivan has requested a trial membership for him and a couple of his men at this club this weekend.

Fuck...

> You can't seriously be considering it?

> DECLAN
>
> We've co-habited for the past six months without a single issue.
>
> And trust me, after everything with Quinn saying that fucking pains me.

RORY

As someone who hates those Russian fucks as much as Declan, I kind of agree.

FINN

Ivan's not that bad. He invited me to Russian Doll a couple of weeks ago when it opened.

DECLAN

You would like a guy that invites you to go look at tits.

FINN

Hey! I might not have gone, but the invite was appreciated.

CONOR

This could forge this alliance between us.

This could be a fucking Trojan horse.

DECLAN

Metal detectors at the door and I say yes.

Easy for you to say... You didn't just make a promise you want to break.

TRISTAN

He plans to bring both his wife and his girlfriend and would like them not to be saddled with our business talk all night.

For fuck's sake...

And we're all agreeing to this? Please tell me we are at least arming our security.

TRISTAN

I might be optimistic that this is a genuine meeting about our families continuing to co-exist.

But I'm definitely not fucking stupid.

Hopefully, you don't have to eat those words...

CHAPTER FORTY-TWO

LIAM

Wearing a strappy red silk dress—made from less fabric than some pocket squares I own—Sasha walks through the club, draped on my arm and drawing the attention of nearly everyone we pass. She's always fucking gorgeous, but the way the dress clings to her curves makes her fucking mesmerizing.

"Thank you, Sir," Sasha purrs in my ear as we wait at the bar to grab a Jameson for me and a glass of bubbly for her. "I know you said we can't play, but can we go down the hall?"

I sip my whiskey and savor the spicy flavor before responding to her. "I didn't say we couldn't play, *mo mhuirnín*. I told you I would not promise to go that far with you." The way her face lights up, you'd think I wasn't filling her pussy every morning, noon, and night. *But exhibitionism hits a little differently*. Even I can't deny that.

"For now, we'll see how you handle being in the hall," I whisper, slipping her hand back into the crook of my arm. She squeezes my bicep with excitement as we walk into the dark. I let her set our leisurely pace, allowing her to choose which rooms we pass and which we pause at to watch the players on the other side.

Sasha's gaze locks on a couple, and our already meandering pace slows to a crawl. On the other side of the sheet of glass, a beautiful blonde is on her knees servicing her Dom. She swallows his impressive length to the base, holding him in her throat as he rains a very skilled Florentine flogger over her arse or upper back.

Sasha lightly chews at her lower lip as we continue to gaze through the window. Shifting her weight, she squeezes her thighs together, trying to quell the need growing between them. "That's fucking hot," she mutters so softly it's almost just a breath.

"It sure fucking is," I whisper, wrapping my arm around her. But I'm not talking about the talented couple she has her eyes on. I'm not observing them. My eyes have been glued to Sasha and enjoying her growing arousal. I pull her back into my chest and let her feel my hard cock against her arse. "Is my dirty girl thinking about how badly she wants to taste my cock?"

"Yes, Sir.

"If I give you what you want"—I pause and run my tongue along the rim of her ear as she watches the man finish on the pretty blonde's face—"are you going to take me down your tight throat and let me cover your tongue with cum?"

She teasingly rubs against my cock, and begs, "Please, Sir." I grab her hand to lead her down the hall, and it is abundantly clear to me that while I might be her Dom, *she* is the one in complete fucking control. With that sweet voice, I'd drop to my knees and feast on her pussy in the middle of Times Square if she asked me to.

When we find an empty room, I swipe my card over the lock and usher her inside. Unbuttoning my shirt and eyeing the floggers hanging on the wall, I command, "Shoes and dress off. Then climb on the lounger and put that sweet arse in the air for me."

She follows my instructions, placing her knees in the dip of the of the tantra chaise and resting her body over the top. Her beautiful round arse juts into the air, and she licks her lips in anticipation of me filling her mouth.

"So fucking eager," I groan, undoing my trousers and freeing my cock. The moment I reach her, she wraps her lips around me and swirls her soft tongue around my sensitive tip. *Fuck that feels good.* I drag the leather strands of the flogger over her bare backside as she worships my cock. She alternates between licking and kissing along my shaft and impressively swallowing me to the hilt, leaving me struggling to safely work the flogger against her.

Her gorgeous chocolate eyes stare up at my body as she forces her lips to the base of my shaft. She holds me deep in the confines of her throat. I increase the intensity of the flogger, and a pleasurable moan rattles from her chest, vibrating along my cock as it constricts her already tight throat. "Fuck!" I grit, fighting back the overwhelming need to prematurely spill down her throat.

"I wish you could see how fucking stunning you are when you swallow my cock," I muse. Sasha pulls from me with a heavy gasp. Her thick spittle dangles from both her lips and my cock, the thread breaking when a smile spreads across her face. "Or how fucking spectacular your arse looks as I paint it red with streaks from my flogger."

Wrapping her lips around my cock again, she stares up at me as she bobs her mouth over my length. *Such a talented fucking tongue...* Her saliva-dampened palms slide over my muscular thighs, and she grips the back of my legs. She opens her mouth and pulls lightly at the back of my thighs. "Are you asking me to fuck your pretty mouth, sweetheart?" I ask, sliding my fingers through her hair and lightly gripping the back of her head.

Her incoherent answer vibrates around my cock. She repeats the vibration, adding a nod to be clear, and I drop the flogger to the floor. "I'll start with your mouth, but I'm going to bury myself down your throat and fuck it raw." I slide my hand along her arm to her hand at the back of my thigh. "If it's too much, pinch me three times because I'm not stopping until I'm ready to fill your mouth."

CHAPTER FORTY-THREE

SASHA

Liam's hand slides from mine, along my arm, and laces through my hair. Cupping the back of my head with both hands, he works himself in and out of my mouth. Slowly at first, but quickly becoming feral, his eyes darken, and his short thrusts grow rapid. His fingers tighten in my locks, and he commands, "Breathe."

I hastily suck in a deep breath, and he chases it down my throat with his cock. My lips crash against his base as he forces me to abruptly swallow every inch of him. His groans and grunts fill the room, his long, deep thrusts not once pulling him from my throat. He throat-fucks me hard, relentlessly thrusting into me until my lungs begin to burn with need for more air. I'm about to pinch his thigh when he retreats to my mouth, just enough to allow me to take a quick breath.

"You. Feel. So. Fucking. Good," Liam grits, driving himself into my throat with every word. His hold in my hair sears my scalp when he flexes his fingers, and I can't stifle the moan that rattles from me. He grows more rigid as the vibrations rise from my lungs, and it's his undoing.

Quickly wrapping his fist around the base of his shaft, he pulls from my throat. He pumps the head of his cock into my mouth a few more times while he fists the base of his shaft. "Fuck!" he roars so loudly when he comes, I'd be surprised if the lounge wasn't notified of his release. His cum shoots over my tongue, and I swallow him down. I lick and suck at his cock until my tongue has washed away every hint of his salty release.

Tucking his spent length back into his pants, Liam walks along the chaise with his fingers dusting along the bare skin of my spine. "They had the pleasure of watching you worship my cock until I came in your mouth," Liam opines, glancing at the sea of people watching from the hall. He quickly returns his full attention to me as he falls to his knees at my feet. "Do you think they deserve to watch as I worship your pussy until you do the same?"

I'm not provided a chance to answer. Liam grips my legs and yanks me down the lounger until my hips are resting on the swell before his face. Tearing my panties to the side, he buries his face into me from behind. "Fuck *mo mhuirnín*," he groans into me. "You taste so fucking good."

Liam's tongue swirls over and around my clit, the groans he makes from the enjoyment he gets pleasuring me matches my moans and whimpers as he expertly works me toward my release. I come fast and hard, my cries of pleasure filling the room when the orgrasm building at my core fires through me. *But it's not enough for him.* Liam wraps his arms around my ass and pulls me into him and the chaise, holding me in place so that he can continue to assault my sensitive clit with his tongue.

"Thank you, Sir," I pant as Liam brings me over the edge once more. He flicks the tip of his tongue against my clit, and I squirm in his tight hold. He rests the tip of his tongue on my clit, then slowly drags it through my pussy, applying more pressure with the flat of his tongue as he licks my entrance. "One more for me."

Darting his tongue into me, Liam tongue-fucks my pussy and licks my clit until my hips are bucking wildly against his face. My clit throbs, and I need him to make me come again as badly as I need him to stop. "Fuck!" It's my turn to cry out. Reaching behind me, I slide my fingers into Liam's hair and fist it tightly. I hold him firmly against me and move my hips to where I need him. He gives me exactly what I need, and I completely unfurl. My orgasm loud, and my release exceptionally wet.

"Good fucking girl," Liam pulls his face from between my thighs, revealing his damp scruff and glistening skin. He rubs his hands along my slick thighs as he makes his way to his feet. A playful half-smirk pulls at the right corner of his mouth, and he teases, "You might be a little too messy to play with in public."

I climb from the chaise as Liam closes the blinds, giving us privacy to clean up and get dressed. After Liam cleans the remnants of his blowjob from my face and my release from my thighs, I slip back into my silky dress. Watching Liam dress, I draw his attention to the rather obvious stain—one of us left—on the thigh of his pants. "Fucking hell," he huffs with a laugh, untucking his shirt.

Liam walks me to the bar and hoists me onto a stool before flagging down Jorge. Garnering his attention, he asks, "By chance, do you have a spare pair of trousers in your locker?"

Jorge nods, fishing in his pocket. "All these years, I've wished for an Evans brother to want to get in my pants..." He sighs, handing Liam his keys. "This really wasn't what I had in mind."

CHAPTER FORTY-FOUR

SASHA

Per Liam's instruction, I keep my "sweet, little red ass parked on this barstool where Jorge can keep an eye on me" while he runs into the back to change his pants.

"*Malen'kaya printsessa*," a deep voice tsks behind me, and I spin to find the same dark-eyed, middle-aged man who approached me at the grocery store a few days ago. He helps himself to the seat beside me and quietly claps his hands. "That was quite the fucking show you put on back there."

I sit beside him silently, trying to hide the reaction he's eliciting. *Sheer fucking panic that my world is about to implode.* The last thing I want is his presence to alert Jorge—or worse—one of Liam's brothers.

"Having *skills* like that though, it's no wonder you convinced that bodyguard of yours to betray his family to run away with you, Alexandra," the man shares his unwelcome, crass thoughts.

Forcing a polite smile, I turn to face him and insist, "I'm sorry, but you must have me confused with someone else. My name is Sasha, not Alexandra. Sasha Martin."

I hold steadfast to my claim, but the man sitting beside me doesn't buy a single syllable of my bullshit. *No, he knows better.*

"Alexandra... Sasha... Or what was it your beloved Viktor called you?" He waves his hands in the air as though he's tossing the names around. His eyes boring through me, he says the name I haven't heard in years. "Sashenka?"

My jaw clenches in anger as sad tears well in my eyes. I can feel myself shaking, and I'm desperately struggling to maintain my composure. Clinging to the idea of trying to convince him that he has the wrong person, I shake my head, "I'm sorry."

He isn't buying it.

"From where you slipped on ice in Saint Petersburg." He lifts his hand from the bar and flicks his fingertip under my jaw, running it over a tiny scar. Dusting the same finger along my elbow, he shares, "From falling off your bike on the Brighton Beach Boardwalk. I believe that happened when you were six."

He doesn't actually know me.

"Who are you?" I snarl under my breath.

"A friend," he states matter-of-factly. "A new-to-you friend, but an old friend of your brother's. He's been searching for you for quite some time."

Six years, two months, and eleven days, if we're going to be exact.

The day Viktor and I took what little we had and quickly ran as far from my family as we could. The day I watched my brother shoot his best friend in the back. The day the man I loved begged me to run as he lay dying face-down in the middle of the street. The day Alexandra Levedeva disappeared without a trace and Sasha Martin was born.

"He's less than pleased to have found you here." The gruff voice draws me back from my thoughts. "Fucking the Irish, of all people, but he is quite happy to finally be able to bring you back home. He's extending an olive branch—as an apology for Viktor—and is giving you the opportunity to leave with me willingly."

"Or what?" I encourage him to finish his threat.

"Or I will leave alone." He shrugs. "I will head outside and face the wrath of your brother. When he's finished with me, he'll come in here with guns blazing—"

"Liam," I mutter, seeing him make his way through the crowd to where I sit.

"Yes, your Liam," the man turns on his barstool and follows my gaze. "Ivan won't hesitate to put a bullet in his skull for touching his *malen'kaya printsessa.*"

His little princess. I scoff. *Rapunzel, that's the closest he ever came to treating me like a princess.* Locking me away in some shitty apartment, keeping me sweet and innocent so he could use me as a bargaining chip. Waiting for the perfect moment to trade his beautiful virginal sister's life to some soulless asshole in exchange for a stake in their family business.

I guess that jokes on me… in exchange for being married off to one soulless asshole, I've been fucked by at least a dozen of them.

"What will it be, Alexandra?" He stands from his barstool and holds his hand for me to join him.

"No," I decline bluntly.

Liam approaches with a furrowed brow and a displeased scowl. He forces himself between me and the man awaiting my hand and wraps his arm around me. Placing a kiss against my temple, clearly marking me as his property, he asks, "Everything okay here?"

"Yes," I fib, forcing a smile. I choose my words carefully not to lie to Liam further. "He saw us down the hall and was very interested in discussing the possibility of me leaving with him."

Liam's eyes narrow, and his nostrils flare at the sheer knowledge another man—who isn't his brother—had the audacity to hit on me.

"And I apologize." Ivan's friend raises both hands in

surrender. "She made it very clear that she wasn't willing to come with me. I was just leaving."

On the exterior, I look calm and collected. But internally, I'm a raging ball of panic. Every fiber of my being screaming, "Tell him!"

"Li—"

"Hey!" Liam shouts at Jorge. Realizing he accidentally cut me off, he mouths *sorry, sweetheart,* before laying into Jorge. "What the fuck? You were supposed to be keeping an eye on her for me." The two of them argue, and my opportunity to tell Liam my truth dwindles with every word the they spit at each other.

"I'm so sorry, *mo mhuirnín,*" Liam apologizes when he finally finishes lambasting Jorge. "What were you going to say?"

Taking a deep breath, I prepare to share the secret I've been holding from him—*from everyone*—for the past six years. Opening my mouth, I expect nervous word-vomit but find silence instead.

He lives in the world you ran from.

He loves you.

He will understand.

"My name... I mean, I—"

CHAPTER FORTY-FIVE

LIAM

Staring up at me, tears well in her eyes, and Sasha stammers, "My name… I mean, I—"

Hearing the all-too-familiar muffled sounds of gunshots, I cut Sasha's words short when I yank her from the barstool and pull her behind me.

I fucking knew it…

I don't need to see Ivan's face to know this is him. *No one—except Finn—would be stupid or crazy enough to pull off shit like this.* For all his bullshit about sharing this city and calling a truce, he wanted nothing more than to earn our trust so that he could infiltrate our lives with ease.

Club members scream, scurrying behind tables and toward emergency exits as a slew of armed men swarm our club. Ivan's Russian accent-laced call billows over them all. "*Malen'kaya printsessa?*"

I've got Sasha firmly wedged between me and the bar to hide her from sight—*and potential gunfire*—with my body.

Drawn guns in hand, Tristan and Declan stalk toward an unfazed Ivan. "I see your word means very little," Tristan gruffly opines, gesturing with the barrel of his gun for Ivan to return to the doors he just entered through.

"My word?" Ivan darkly laughs, his gaze leisurely wandering around the club as he walks further into it. Grabbing a recently vacated stool at the other end of the bar, he sits and helps himself to the freshly poured beer left behind.

Sasha fists the fabric of my shirt and buries her face into my back, further shielding herself from Ivan and his men. Reaching behind me, I place my hand on her hip and find her trembling. I squeeze her—silently trying to let her know that I'll do everything I can to keep her safe—as I turn slightly to further conceal her from the men gathering beside Ivan.

Tapping the muzzle of his gun on the bar, Ivan sincerely comments, "This is a nice fucking place you've got here."

"Thanks," Declan deadpans.

"And filled with such gorgeous fucking women." Ivan's looks around the room as he speaks. He's looking for something or someone. "Pretty sure we all could have had a good time here, sharing some of these beauties. It's a fucking shame you broke our agreement."

"Funny, I don't think it's us who have just barged into your strip club," I snark. "But we are the ones that broke the truce between us?"

"We agreed I would stay out of your business and you would stay out of mine," Ivan reminds, staring back at me with anger. His stare is unwavering, and his nostrils flare with every heated breath he takes. He sure as fuck thinks we—*or I*—did something.

Ivan continues to glare at me as Tristan tries to calm the situation, "I assure you we have held our end of the agg—"

"No!" Ivan interrupts Tristan with a roar, the heated flush of anger creeping up his tattooed neck as he slams the butt of his gun against the bar with enough force to chip the marble. He takes a second to get a grip on his anger and finally breaks our stare to return his attention to Tristan. "Do you not know what goes on in your own house? Is that how you run your operation?"

Tristan shakes his head, still as oblivious to Ivan's ranting outburst as the rest of us. Ivan slides from his stool and calmly finishes the beer he helped himself to. Walking toward Tristan and Declan, he glances in my direction and snarks, "You might need to confirm that with the rest of your brothers."

Sasha lets out a soft, whimpered sigh from behind me and I squeeze her hip, praying she stays quiet and doesn't draw his attention. I don't get my wish, and he snaps his head to me, his narrowed eyes even more angry than before.

"I have spent a very long time looking for something that belongs to me. Years of hard work and anguish trying to find it. Scouring this city and our fucking homeland. Imagine my surprise to finally find it right under my fucking nose," Ivan rants, pushing past Tristan and Declan as he makes his way toward me.

Sasha trembles harder against my back with every step Ivan takes in my direction, and it pains me beyond words that I can't do anything to comfort her in this moment without further risking her safety.

Reaching me, Ivan condescendingly taps the barrel of his gun against my chest and asks, "Are you in the habit of keeping things that don't belong to you?"

Under any other circumstances, I would risk the bullet he might fire—and those of his *comrads*—to beat the piss out of him where he stands for daring to threaten me. But this are different. A bullet could easily pass through my body and into Sasha's. And that isn't a risk I am remotely willing to take.

All my brothers stare at me, each of them as blind to my crime as I am. I return their stare with a tiny shrug and a shake of my head.

"I thought I was very clear that if you fucked with me, the truce we made would be over." Ivan stands toe-to-

toe with me and presses the muzzle of his gun against my jaw. "And *you* have most definitely stuck your *manky* Irish cocks where they don't belong."

The muzzle grinds beneath my chin, and he seethes, "Normally, I would've already rained your fucking brains across this bar. But I'm trying to extend a fucking olive branch here."

A fucking olive branch? Really? **This** *is his fucked-up version of a peace offering.*

"*Malen'kaya printsessa,*" he exhales, his tone softening but still dark and gravelly. "I just want what's mine. This doesn't have to be like last time."

"Last time?" I ask in confusion, only to have my question ignored.

"If I get what belongs to me, no one has to die tonight," Ivan promises, and Sasha's hands slip from my shirt. My skin vibrates as she mutters against my back, but she's so quiet I can't make out what she's saying.

She slides from between me and the bar, putting herself in clear view—and danger—of Ivan. His eyes light up the second he sees her, and my stomach flops with terror. She takes a step toward him, and I grasp for her arm. "Sasha, what the fuck are you do—"

"*Malen'kaya printsessa,*" Ivan sighs delightfully, a relieved smile pulling at the side of his mouth. He grips her jaw with his free hand, and I snarl as he uses the hold to drag her toward him. Dipping his head, he places a chaste kiss against her lips. Not relinquishing her face as he stands, he whispers, "Alexandra... I've missed you, little sister."

<h1 style="text-align:center">CHAPTER FORTY-SIX</h1>

LIAM

Ivan holds Sasha's face in one hand and shoves his gun firmly against my chest with the other. I stand dumbfounded, frozen in place, trying to comprehend his words. *I've missed you, little sister.* Trying to comprehend anything.

Sasha doesn't resist in the slightest as Ivan protectively slides his arm around her shoulders and possessively tugs her into him. Even as I watch things unfold, I can't seem to get my brain to register what Ivan said.

I've missed you, little sister.

"You always were remarkably deceptive, Alexandra"—Ivan's praise and the name he uses quickly pulls Sasha's attention from the floor to his face—"but it appears you have *completely* fucking fooled this one. You've fooled me before, but this... This is fucking impressive. He's fucking speechless."

I can barely think... let alone string together enough words to say something.

Ivan erupts with a short, dark laugh and shakes his head as he turns his attention back to me. "You poor Irish bastard. You really had no idea who she was, did you? Were you blinded by her pussy? Or was she really that fucking believable?"

Sasha doesn't say a word—or so much as glance in my direction—as Ivan leads her from the club. His men follow shortly behind him, and they all step out of the front door of the club. And she's gone. Walking out of my life as quickly as she crashed into it.

I can't fucking breathe. The walls are closing in. My entire fucking world is imploding.

This was far worse than Sasha simply leaving me. The two of them mocking me and throwing the last couple of months in my face like it was a fucking joke. Worse than a joke. *It was all a fucking lie.* Every word. Every touch. Every fucking moment. The years of barriers I tore down, the things I allowed myself to feel. *For her.* All of it was nothing more than a carefully constructed lie. And me, nothing more than the fucking *plonker* who believed it.

Rage bubbling inside me, I grab the nearest thing I can find. I hurl the stool over the bar and into the wall of liquor bottles behind it, every emotion pouring from me in a thunderous roar. The satisfaction of it exploding against the wall and shattering the bottles to the floor is fleeting. And not nearly enough to fill the gaping hole that Sasha just left in my chest. I grab the next thing I can reach—a half-drunk bottle of Guinness—and chuck it toward the broken bottles spilling over the back bar.

Storming the length of the bar, I toss every glass or bottle I can get my hands on. Throwing them all, I watch them shatter across the floor. *Like every dream I had for the two of us.* I was going to fucking marry her... Instead of a wife, I'm left with nothing but a hollow version of the truth.

The truth.

Ha!

I try to remember everything. *What the fuck did I miss?* Every little detail she ever shared about herself... her past... her family... what she felt for me... how **we** were the first good thing she's ever had.

Was any of it fucking real?

My heart slams against my chest, the rage continuing to swell far beyond what my body can contain. The white-hot fury coursing through me doesn't care about what was real. The fury just wants to tear everything apart. And for a moment, I let it. Pure anger is the only thing keeping me from completely fucking falling apart. I've never been so fucking furious in my entire life. Not just at her, but at myself for being so fucking stupid. So fucking naïve.

Never again... I fucking knew better.

"Why?" I shout—my voice so hoarse it sounds foreign —as I throw another barstool. It clatters across the marble floor, doing nothing to release the tension building inside me. It isn't enough. None of it is enough.

Nothing will ever be enough to fill the void she just left where my soul once was.

My entire body trembles, and my heart pounds so hard that it's going to burst from my heaving chest. Anger consumes me, and I don't know how to stop it. All I want is to make her feel an ounce of this gut-wrenching betrayal, but she is gone. And I'm left with emotions I don't know how to deal with. I don't know how to let them go. *How to let **her** go.*

I slam my fist into the marble bar top, the radiating pain of the impact momentarily grounding me. The anger clawing at me and tearing me apart begins to fade. It subsides into something worse. Something much harder to face...

Heartache.

It's the last thing I want to feel. *The one thing I promised myself I'd never experience again.* I kick the tattered barstool at my feet and roar as I toss another. I rage and scream, not willing to give into everything else I'm feeling. The club surrounding me is a war zone, and I stand in the middle of the mess I've created, shaking my head as my body tires and the anger subsides.

Left with nothing but the pieces of a life I thought I knew, I fall apart. My legs falter beneath me, and I crumble to the floor, as broken as the shattered glass I land in.

"Fuck, Li…" Declan sighs, wrapping his arms around me as he kneels in the glass beside me. My brothers all huddle around me, letting me grieve with only the sounds of my heaving breath in the room. Each of them prepared to pick me up and help me piece my life back together when I'm ready.

CHAPTER FORTY-SEVEN
SASHA

One of Ivan's goons shoves me into the back of the G-Class as Ivan climbs in the other side.

"You didn't have to do that," I mutter, my broken heart slamming against my ribs. It didn't have to happen like that. He didn't need to hurt Liam like that. But my brother always has had a way of stealing everything good from me. *Always.*

Ivan would've killed Liam—*like he killed Viktor*—to bring me back home. I knew giving Ivan what he wanted would spare the life of the man I love; I just didn't realize how hard it would be. *Or how much it would hurt.* Liam's face was filled with so much grief and confusion. The weight of seeing my betrayal in his eyes was suffocating.

He trusted me, and I lied to him.

He loved me, and I failed him.

But I hadn't lied, not like Ivan made it sound. What he did was beyond cruel. It was twisted.

I am the person he thought I was.

"You're fucking Bratva, *malen'kaya printsessa*," Ivan huffs. "*This* is where you belong."

"That might be, but you didn't need to make him think that I did this for you." I shake my head. "You might not have killed him, like Viktor, but you fucking destroyed him."

"Good." The elongated word spills from the side of his mouth as he lights a cigarette. He takes a long drag on it and expels the smoke through his nostrils. "That means he'll want nothing to do with you. You deserve better than being showcased like their little Russian whore."

"Like what?" I scoff. "Being the Russian whore whose virginity you can auction off to the highest bidder or the one you can marry off like property to make a business arrangement with some disgusting old man."

"No, *malen'kaya printsessa*. You give yourself too much credit." Ivan evilly chuckles. "You lost a lot of fucking value when you gave your fucking virtue to a lowly bodyguard. Now it'd be like selling off one of the well-worn cunts at the club. I'd be lucky to pay off a bet with a used-up slut like you."

"I loved him," I exhale, shaking my head and ignoring his insults. "And Viktor was your best fucking friend."

"*Was*," Ivan sternly corrects me. "That was before he thought he had the right to fuck you."

Who guns down their best friend in cold blood for falling in love with their little sister?

"You're a fucking psychotic prick," I snarl.

Ivan grips my face and squeezes my cheeks so hard I almost wince before grumbling, "And you've become a mouthy fucking bitch since I saw you last."

"You're still the same asshole, though," I spit, freeing myself from his tight hold.

The conviction to stand toe-to-toe with any man... When Liam said it, I never thought that man would be my unhinged, narcissistic brother.

———

Lying in bed, I press my hands to my eyes and try to hold back the tears, but it's useless. It's been two days, and they continue to relentlessly fall from my eyes, cascading down my cheeks so much they sting. I wrap my arms around my knees and pull them tightly to my chest, staring blankly out of the small window as tears start to blur my vision once more.

The hardest part of all of this is that Liam believed Ivan. There was no hiding his rage as it visibly flared up his neck and over his face.

I had secrets. Things that were messy and complicated, things I hadn't wanted to share with him yet. Sordid details from my past that I wasn't ready to deal with. I wasn't ready to open up that much to anyone, to expose the raw, unhealed parts of my heart. The parts of me that Liam was slowly putting back together.

But that didn't mean I was lying to him. It didn't mean I wasn't real with him. I might not have told him my real name, where I came from, or who my family was, but I was myself with Liam. The person I was with him —*the one he fell in love with*—was real. Everything about *us* was real.

And now it's over...

If only I had gathered the courage to tell him sooner... He would've been hurt, but not like this. He could've forgiven me. But the way he found out—*what Ivan made him believe*—was a total betrayal and shattered any trust he had in me.

And it's my fault.

Curling into a ball, I pull my legs tighter to my chest in the hopes my arms might actually help hold me together. But it's futile. Tears continue to stream down my face and dampen the pillow they fall on as every breath I take suffocates me.

I've lost everything...

I wipe my tears, but it does nothing to stop them. I've cried so many tears since the club that my eyes are raw and swollen. I've spent the last six years of my life enduring atrocious pain, but nothing any of those men did to me hurts like this. This is different. This is deep and all-consuming. It is the kind of agony that leaves me questioning if a life without Liam is even a life worth living.

I need him... I need Liam.

He makes me feel like I am worth something; like I matter. He makes me realize I am worthy of being loved. *Of **him** loving me.*

My heart feels like it's shredding into thousands of pieces. I can still feel his hands on my skin. The way he whispered my name in my ear with love and adoration. And the soft promises of a lifetime together as I fell asleep in his arms. The life he wanted to give me.

The life I wanted to live with him.

Everything I wanted—and had—is now a bittersweet dream, while I'm thrust back into the nightmare I ran from. All alone once again with a gaping emptiness in my chest as my entire life comes to a crashing halt.

It's been a week. Seven agony-laced days since I last saw Sasha or had the warmth of her body curled against mine. I can still hear her sweet laugh and the way she said my name like I was the only person who mattered. It's funny how time can feel so long and so short at the same time. It feels like I've been without her for an eternity.

Our time together might have been nothing more than a string of lies, but it doesn't make what I've lost hurt any less. The pain is still fresh. It leaves me numb, lying in our bed for hours on end, staring at the ceiling, and trying to find what I missed. Searching desperately for everything I should have seen coming.

But there's nothing... Everything about her was fucking perfect.

"Liam?" Declan's deep voice echoes around my empty apartment. The soles of his shoes slap along the hardwood floor of the hallway as he walks toward my bedroom.

"I said I'm fine," I gruff when he pokes his head through the door.

"Maybe, but you look like fucking shit." He walks into the room with Quinn on his heel.

"Jesus, Li…" she exhales, taking in my unusually disheveled appearance. Grabbing the blankets at the foot of the bed, she hesitates for a second. "Am I going to see more than I'm bargaining for?"

"Not likely," Declan answers for me, wiggling his pinky in the air. "He's the runt of the litter, if you catch my drift."

"Fuck you," I spit, sitting up and throwing back the covers to lunge at Declan.

"I've seen bigger, but it's not bad." Quinn winks at me, throwing a pillow at me to cover myself.

"It's good to see you've some fucking fight left in you," Declan quips, walking into the bathroom and turning on the shower.

Storming after him, holding the pillow to cover myself from Quinn, I growl, "What the fuck are you doing?"

"Returning the fucking favor." He grabs the pillow and shoves me under the icy spray of the shower. I grumble and try to jump from the stream, but he shoves me back under. "You forced me to pick up the pieces of my life when I was at my lowest. I'm not going to let you lay here for weeks on end and wallow in your grief."

"Besides, you're being a fucking idiot," Quinn chirps, letting herself into the bathroom. "You know that, right?"

"Fucking hell!" I exclaim, slapping my hands over my cock. I'm generally not modest—*I fuck in public, for Christ's sake*—but it's Quinn. For all the flirting and jokes about sleeping with her, I respect my brother way too much to have my cock swinging in her presence. "Can this conversation wait a minute or two?"

"Nope." She hops onto the bathroom vanity across from the shower, also to Declan's dismay. Looking between us both with a shrug, she sasses, "What? It's not like I haven't seen it already."

"Really?" I snark, glaring at Declan with a furrowed brow. Of all my brothers, I would have expected him to possessively carry her from the room over his shoulder.

Instead, he crosses his arms and leans against the shower stall, looking like he's ready to beat the piss out of me or knock some sense into me. "You're a fucking idiot."

I don't want to talk about this... With either of them. *Especially not while I'm naked and holding my cock.* Even if I was clothed, I'm not ready for this pep talk.

"I don't want to hear it," I mutter, releasing my cock in hopes it gets at least one of them to leave. *Stoic like fucking statues.* Grabbing the soap, I huff, "Just let me be."

"I get it," Declan tells me with a slow, empathetic sigh. "You're hurting."

I shake my head, trying not to let thoughts of her slip back in. "You don't understand," I scoff. "It wasn't real. None of it was real."

"Bull-fucking-shit!" Quinn challenges from her perch. "It's not your heart that's broken, it's your fucking pride. Because you know damn well that is not even the slightest bit true."

Fuck, Quinn...

"The two of you of you were good together. For *each other*. You love her, and she loves you." Quinn seriously doesn't know when to stop.

I hate this. I hate it because part of me knows that she's right. I *do* love Sasha.

"It was a lie," I insist, rinsing the suds from my body down the drain.

"She lied," Quinn admits, shaking her head while looking at me like I'm the idiot she keeps claiming I am. "But the two of you weren't a lie. What did I say to you the night I first met her?"

I think back for a second. "That you'd never seen me so happy."

"That was *real*. The way she looked at you to elicit a smile like that... It was real," Quinn insists, sliding from the counter as I turn off the water, and tosses me a towel. "So, she didn't tell you who she was. Did you ever stop to think that maybe she had a good reason?"

"She messed up. So what?" Declan adds. "Relationships are fucking messy. You fuck up and you fix it."

"You don't behave like a fucking idiot," Quinn chimes.

"You go after her. You fucking fight for her." Turning his attention to Quinn with an apologetic smile, Declan insists, "You don't just let her slip away because it's fucking hard."

"I don't even know if she *wants* me to fucking fight for her." My words carry every bit of bitterness I've been harboring for the past week. The betrayal of having Sasha walk out of my life, I can get over that. *Eventually.* Staring into her eyes and having to endure her confirming I meant nothing to her... No, that will fucking break me.

"She needs you to fight," Quinn imparts confidently. "Don't be a fucking coward—"

"Now I'm an idiot *and* a coward," I tease with a hint of sarcasm, pulling on a pair of trousers.

Smiling at the first light-hearted thing I've said in a week, Quinn continues, "Just don't let your foolish pride get in the way of something and some*one* that matters."

"Don't sit around on your arse and spend the rest of your life regretting it." Declan places his hand on my shoulder and gives it a fatherly squeeze.

I don't respond as I finish dressing and put on my shoes. I'm not sure if I'll regret listening to them. I'm not sure about much of anything right now. But I know with certainty I'm already lost without her. And I'll stay that way if I don't try.

"Did you two draw the short straw?" I ask. "Or did the others vote you two because you could guilt me with all your trauma?"

"Does it matter?" Quinn quips with a smile, handing me the keys to my car.

CHAPTER FORTY-NINE

SASHA

My prison is a luxury penthouse shared with the man who has repeatedly ruined my life. This place is vast and sprawling, yet it feels like the walls are constantly closing in on me. Ivan's laugh echoes through the open space, and it sickens me. He's always had a way of getting inside my head and making me feel like I have no choice but to obey him. That I'm small and powerless.

I'm not that scared little girl anymore.

"You aren't leaving, Alexandra," Ivan insists. My heart pounding, and my mind racing, I clench my fists at my sides as Ivan paces the room before me. "And it's not like your Irish"—he air quotes—"*boyfriend* is coming to rescue you."

As usual, his words are filled with a deadly venom. His entire motive is to provoke me. It always is. He gets off on the reactions he pulls from me... *From everyone.*

"I don't need rescuing, Ivan," I snip, trying to hide the nerves and fear bubbling within me. "I just need you to let me go."

"Let you go?" Ivan scoffs, stopping before me. Gripping my chin, he yanks my face up to his and stares down at me with cold, dark eyes. "Do you really think that after spending all those years trying to find you I'm going to let you simply walk out of here? You're my sister, Alexandra. You belong to me."

His words and the possessiveness in his tone cause bile to pool in my throat. Since father—*even before*—he's thought he has some sort of claim over me. "I don't belong to you," I softly exhale, shaking my head. "You've never *owned* me. I'm not your property. I'm your sister, not some token or bargaining chip for you to use at your will."

He closes what little distance there is between us until his face is just inches from mine. His breath—laced with cigarette smoke and vodka—wafts over me as he lets out an evil, cold laugh.

"You really think you'd live happily ever after with *him*?" Ivan snickers. "We only get death and betrayal in our world, *malen'kaya printsessa*. We don't get happily ever afters."

His brothers have. *We could, too.* Living happily for whatever time we have together would be better than nothing. *Better than this.*

"That man you think so highly of, who you think loves you so much, he hasn't even tried to contact you." Ivan's words hit like a punch to the gut. *Because he's right.* It's been a week. If Liam really loved me, he would've come for me by now. He would have tried to reach out. *Wouldn't he?*

"You don't know him," I mumble, hoping I actually do know Liam Evans as I think I do.

Ivan's dark eyes glimmer, knowing he has finally touched a nerve. "I know enough. If I cared for anyone the way you *think* he cares about you, I would have barged in here, guns blazing, to save you. But he hasn't come to rescue the woman he loves because this isn't a fucking fairy tale."

I gulp, trying to swallow the doubt Ivan is causing to build inside me. "You're wrong," I retort, my conviction becoming weaker by the minute as Ivan's seeds of doubt continue to germinate.

"Don't fool yourself, Alexandra." Ivan shakes his head, his devilish grin still mocking me. "He doesn't love you the way you think he does."

Trying to ignore Ivan's encroaching thoughts, I dig for the strength Liam has worked so hard to instill in me. The confidence to be strong and outspoken. To stand toe-to-toe with any man. Meeting Ivan's gaze, I pull myself straighter and refuse to give in to him. "You don't know Liam. Or his family. You don't know what they'd do for him. *For me.* I won't allow you to make me doubt that."

Ivan stares back at me, the cockiness fading from his smirk, but he doesn't ease up. "You can lie to yourself all you want, but it doesn't matter… You're going to have a long mafia life with the Bratva. Where you *belong,* as you help me forge the empire our father wanted."

Before I can respond, we're interrupted by a loud commotion outside the penthouse. My breath hitches as I turn toward where it is coming from. I don't need the door to open to know who is on the other side. *Liam.* For the first time in seven excruciatingly long days, I feel something other than a painful emptiness in my chest. *Hope.*

The door flies open, and Liam stands on the other side. Gun in hand, his jaw is clenched tight, and his eyes are full of worry and rage. He looks nothing like the calm, collected, and patient man I'm used to. This man looks like he is readying to walk through hell. *For me.*

Ivan doesn't move, and for a moment, I think he might actually not react to the unfolding situation. But his face hardens, and his naturally dark eyes fill with anger. He pulls the gun from the back of his pants and lifts it toward Liam.

"Liam," I shriek, expecting him to meet the same fate as Viktor with visions of his lifeless body falling to the floor flashing through my mind.

His eyes lock on mine, and I immediately get the reassurance I need as he whispers, "*Mo mhuirnín.*"

And in this moment, I know... Ivan's words don't matter.

Liam still loves me.

CHAPTER FIFTY
LIAM

When I see Sasha, I don't need her to speak a word to confirm what Quinn was so certain of. Whatever lies Sasha told and the reasons she had for doing so don't matter. *Sasha fucking loves me.*

"I'm surprised to see you here, Liam," Ivan grits, his voice smooth and controlled. His jaw is clenched, and his eyes are cold and calculating. They flicker to Sasha and back to me. I don't know what he's thinking, but the air is growing heavier with every second that passes.

Taking a step forward, I hold his pitch-black stare. "You knew I'd come. And I'm not leaving until I get what I want."

"And *what* is that?" he asks with a raised brow, knowing damn well *who* I want.

"Sasha," I state matter-of-factly, not interested in playing mindfuck games with him.

"And you think I'm just going to give her to you?" His words hold no emotion.

"She's nothing more than a pawn in a game to you, Ivan. We all know it. You think you can control her... But you can't. You don't know Sasha like I do. She's not the kind of woman you can demand control of."

Not anymore.

Lowering my gun, I walk toward the two of them. "I'm not here to negotiate. I'm here to give you exactly what you want."

Ivan stares back at me with a raised brow. "What I want?" he mocks me. "How could you have any idea what I want?"

"I'll give you what you want," I repeat myself. "Half of everything I have. My family's empire. The wealth. The power. *Everything.*"

His smirk falters for just a moment, but he recovers quickly, narrowing his eyes with uncertainty. "Half of your family's *empire?*" he echoes me, as though testing the words on his tongue. "You expect me to believe you'd give it up for a woman whose name you don't even know?"

"Sasha Martin," I challenge, my voice unwavering. "Sasha Evans when I marry her and merge our families. Our territories. Our businesses. We'll combine everything. You'll have all our resources and muscle at your fingertips. We'll be stronger together, and you'll have more fucking power than you could wield on your own."

His gaze shifts slightly, a flicker of interest as his eyes dart between me and Sasha. He isn't fucking stupid. He knows what I'm offering.

Power. Control. Respect.

"I told you I wasn't here to negotiate," I affirm, my voice low and firm. I was at a disadvantage the minute I saw Sasha's face. I'll do whatever it takes to have a chance with her again. Half our empire is nothing compared to having her in my arms. *Although, my brothers might disagree when they find out.* But I'd give Ivan fucking everything if he demanded it for a life with Sasha.

"Liam," Sasha mutters under her breath. "You can't do that for me."

"It's done, *mo mhuirnín.*"

Ivan studies me for a long moment, and I can see the wheels turning as he weighs his options. The tension between us is thick and palpable. He takes a step closer, his breath hot on my face. I breathe in his smoke-tainted breath as he tries to retain a semblance of the upper hand. "You think I'll just let you walk away with her, don't you?"

"We *are* making a deal, or one of us isn't walking out of this room," I clarify, not backing down. "And one of us has four brothers who will be seeking much more than revenge if it's me who doesn't."

Ivan's eyes flicker for a moment, a brief flash of uncertainty. I don't know whether it's excitement about what I'm offering or that he's contemplating if he's as ready to die for his sister as I am. Maybe it's because the one thing he can't control is what I'm willing to sacrifice everything for. While he hesitates, I know with certainty that I would lay down my life for her. *She's my fucking family.*

Ivan steps back, running his fingers through his dark hair. He lets out a long breath, and for a moment, the heavy weight of the room seems to lift.

"If you're really serious about this, then you need to prove it," Ivan announces. "You marry her within the week and provide proof of our bonded blood within the year."

An heir?

My chest tightens at the finality of his demand. I'd do anything to have Sasha in my life, including happily fathering a fucking baseball team like Declan. I want to agree to his terms, but I can't.

"I can't agree to that, Ivan." I shake my head. His face sours as I turn my attention to Sasha and find the devastation in her eyes. "I love you far too much to force that upon you, *mo mhuirnín*. It's not my decision to make. It's yours."

"Yes," she blurts without hesitation, tears already falling down her face.

"Then go." Ivan lowers his gun, his face beaming with satisfaction at the deal. "But remember, Liam, you're playing a dangerous fucking game. If you fail... If you break our deal, I will make sure you and your brothers regret it once and for all."

I don't turn my attention to him. Every ounce of my being is focused on the one thing I came here for. The one thing I want—the one *person* I *need*—more than anything else in this world. Holding her gaze with unwavering intensity, I promise, "I won't fail."

CHAPTER FIFTY-ONE
SASHA

Our reunion isn't filled with passionate kisses and lingering embraces. Ours is clouded with the painful weight of the secrets I kept from Liam. Secrets that have cost him half of what he and his family have spent decades building.

Standing beside Liam in the elevator, my heart races, and my hands wring at the front of my floral midi dress. I can barely bring myself to lift my face to look him in the eye.

He stands across from me—hands tucked into the pockets of his pants—with a steady gaze, waiting. Waiting for me to speak. Giving me the opportunity, he knows I need to make this right.

The guilt has gnawed at me since I fell for him. This past week has been crushing. I hadn't told him the truth, even with hundreds of opportunities to do so.

"I'm sorry," I whisper, barely above a breath. "I should've told you. I should've told you from the start."

Liam doesn't move from where he stands a few feet before me. The distance and his silence are almost unbearable. But he deserves to know. *I need to get it out.* It's been eating me alive for far too long, and it nearly destroyed us. I need him to understand.

"I wasn't honest with you," I continue, my words tumbling out. Needing to say them before I lose my nerve and desperate for him to hear me. "I... I lied to you. About everything. About who I was. About my name. About where I came from. All of it. I didn't tell you because—"

"Because you were ashamed?" he finishes for me, his voice low but steady. His eyes flicker, like he is trying to piece together the fragments of an incomplete puzzle. "Sasha..."

The way he says my name makes my chest ache.

I've missed it so much.

I nod, not trusting myself to speak without collapsing with anguished tears. Every word I just spoke was already falling short of explaining the real truth—the shame, the fear, the desperation to escape the very arrangement he just made with my brother.

His expression softens. For a moment, I swear I see a moment of understanding. It's fleeting and gone as quickly as it came, replaced by something else. Something I can't quite read.

"You don't get it, do you?" he whispers. "None of that matters to me. None of it."

"I thought if you knew…"—my voice shakes as I struggle to control my emotions—"if you knew who I was… Who I *really* was. That my brother would come for you… That you would have sent me away. And then, when I realized I had fallen in love with you… I was terrified you wouldn't love me anymore."

"No, *mo mhuirnín*." Liam slowly shakes his head. "It doesn't matter. It's never mattered."

I open my mouth, but the look in his eyes silences me. There is no judgment. No fear. No resentment. Just something raw and unfettered.

"Don't you get it?" His voice is deep but gentle. The intensity of it shakes me to my core. "It doesn't matter. I love you. Even when I didn't want to… When I tried to keep my distance… When you broke my heart and I tried to hate you. I couldn't. I'm so fucking consumed with love for you that I don't fucking care."

Tears well in my eyes, and I flutter my lids, trying to keep them at bay. "Li…"

"I don't care who you were. I don't care what your name used to be. Or where you came from. I fell in love with *you*. Not the woman you were supposed to be or the one you think you need to be. I love the one you were when you were with me. The one standing before me fighting back tears. That's the only one that matters to me. You, Sasha..."

I step backward, the cold metal of the elevator cab pressing against my back. My knees are trembling, and I grip the metal rail behind me to steady myself. "You still love me?" I choke.

He stares back at me—his lips slightly parted—with his gaze softening. "I demanded your hand in marriage with a gun in my face." He chuckles. "Of course I still love you. That hasn't changed. Not now. Not ever, *mo mhuirnín.*"

I close my eyes, the weight of his words settling over me. His hands—gentle but firm—pull me into him. I crash into his hard body with a thud, and his lips are immediately pressed against mine. "I love you," he says through our kiss.

He claims my mouth until I'm breathless. I pull back to take a breath. "I love you."

"I know." He smirks, crashing his lips back into mine. His hands slide down my body and over the curve of my ass. He gives it a firm squeeze and pulls me from the ground. My legs wrap instinctually around him as the doors of the elevator open.

My chest heaving, I stare at him and bite my lower lip, "Sir?"

Liam's eyes dart between me and the parking garage on the other side of the doors as his hand slides through my hair. He lets out a pained sigh. "I'm trying to decide if I can make it to the car before I need to be inside you."

The elevator doors begin to slide shut, and I giggle. "Nope."

CHAPTER FIFTY-TWO
LIAM

I slam Sasha's back into the icy wall of the elevator with a thud before the doors finish closing. She claws at the skirt of her dress tucked between us as I fumble with the belt and zipper of my trousers. Freeing my cock, I tear her panties to the side and stare into her eyes as I slide into her.

"I'll worship you like you deserve when we get home," I pant into the side of her neck as I plunge my cock into her. "But right now... I need to make sure you know you're mine."

I drive my cock into her fast and deep, grunting as I repeatedly bottom out inside of her. Her legs flex around me, and sweet whimpers spew from her with every brutal thrust.

"God, I fucking missed you." I kiss along her neck. While sloppily claiming her mouth, I increase the speed of my hips until my savage thrusts fill the small cab with our primitive moans and cries. Her tight cunt quivers around me, and I know she's teetering on the edge. I'm not far behind. "Come for me, sweetheart. I need to feel you squeezing around me when I come."

"Yes... Sir..." Sasha painfully replies. I palm her ass and bury the entirety of my cock in her, and she cries out in sheer bliss.

"Fuck," I grit, sliding through her quivering cunt and spilling my release into her. Sinking into her a final time, I still when I'm buried to hilt and relish in the feel of her trembling around me as I taste her sweet lips. Pulling back with a smirk, I whisper, "If your pussy is going to milk my fucking cock like this, I'm going to make due on my promise in no time."

———

I never thought I'd find myself in this position. Standing in front of my brothers with a heavy heart, knowing that everything we've worked for—sacrificed and spilled blood for—has gone. And that I would've given so much more to get back what I wanted.

I didn't know how to begin to tell them. We've been through hell and back together more times than I could list. This life, we've built it together. Every decision we've made has been with all of us in mind because it wasn't about *any* of us. It has always been about *all* of us. What I did was different. It wasn't business. It wasn't for my brothers. It was for *her*.

Meeting them in the lounge, the weight of the deal I made with Ivan sits heavy on my shoulders. I don't need to say anything. The way they are looking at me, they know something is wrong.

"Spit it out, Liam," Tristan gruffs, his usually calm demeanor replaced with a sharp bite. He shifts in his seat. "What did you do?"

Fuck... That tone is generally reserved for Finn and the unhinged shit he does without thinking.

I swallow, the words caught in the back of my throat. "I gave it away." My voice is flat, almost numb, as I look at my brothers. They all glare back at me in silence, glancing at each other, trying to comprehend what I have just said.

"Gave it away?" Declan repeats me, his brow furrowing as if he didn't hear me correctly.

Running my hand through my hair, I try to find the right words. But there aren't any. How do you explain to your brothers that you have given away the thing that defines you and has been the biggest part of your lives so you can have a chance at love?

"I gave our empire to Ivan," I blurt. *Nope, those definitely weren't the right words.* "Not all of it. Half: Merging our families when I marry Sasha."

"You what?" Conor's voice booms over the grumblings of my brothers.

"Quinn and I told you not to be a fucking idiot. To go and get her back," Declan scoffs. "Not to give him everything we've built like a *fucking idiot.*"

Tristan stares at me over his glass as he leans back in his chair. "Merging our families with his is no small thing, Liam. It comes with a price. And I'm not just talking about money or territory."

"I know." My eyes meet his, filled with the understanding of the gravity of my decision. "I love her. I love Sasha. So much that I don't give a fuck about rivalry, about power. *About anything.* I want to be with her. And I'll do whatever it takes to make that happen."

There is a long pause as my brothers exchange glances, considering what I said. They are weighing the risks, the consequences, and what this decision means for all of us. *Something I probably should have done before impulsively throwing the option on the table.*

"I don't know what the lot of you are grumbling about." Finn breaks the silence. "We'd all do the same for Layla, Quinn or Cat. Well, I probably would've fucking shot him, but that's a me problem."

Declan rolls his eyes at Finn's confession, but none of them argue with him. They aren't angry. Not one of them is condemning me for so recklessly making this decision without them. Instead, they're giving me the two things I should've expected. *Unwavering loyalty and support.*

"We've all been there," Tristan exhales. "Not in the same way, and not giving away half our empire... But we've all had to make sacrifices for the people we love. I have for Layla. And Declan—"

"I don't need to tell you what I'd do for Quinn or my kids," Declan interrupts. "And all of you were at my side when I did it. We were there for Finn when Catlin needed us. We'll be there for you, even if this is fucking stupid."

"I stood by them, and I'll stand by you," Conor announces. "I mean, I'd rather get shot than give away everything *and* have to work with the fucking Russians, but you're my brother. If that's what you needed to do to bring her home, I get it. *Rud ar bith do mo dheartháir.*"

"We all get it." Finn shrugs.

"But I'm going to count the portion I'm apparently giving to Ivan as a down payment on the unlimited wanks I'm going to have thinking about Sasha," Conor taunts.

"Deal!" Declan, Tristan, and Finn chorus.

EPILOGUE
SASHA

It's hard to believe that it's been six months already. Six months since a whirlwind engagement and me walking out of Our Lady of Grace as his wife. Sasha Evans. Bound not only to Liam and our new life, but the new life for our families.

I glance up from my book to find Liam by the fireplace, his gaze fixated on me. The soft glow of the sunset filtering through the windows is reflected in his eyes. The way he looks at me—always like he's seeing me for the first time—causes my heart to race.

He crosses the room and drags his fingers along the edge of my jaw, smiling softly. Liam stands before me with an air of power and authority—as my Sir. But also, as *my* Liam. The man who promised to heal the broken parts of me and has upheld his word more than I'll ever be able to express.

"I want to play, *mo mhuirnín*," Liam whispers with a deep growl. He pulls me from the couch and into his body. "You have two minutes to get your sweet ass in the playroom. I expect you ready when I get there." The second he lets go of me, I scurry down the hall, unable to control my excited giggle.

Stripping off my clothes as I walk through the door, I grab a heavy wooden paddle from the wall. I carry it back to the door, take a breath, and lower myself to the floor. Legs slightly parted with the paddle resting on them, I press my knees into the floor and bow my head. I do so willingly—*eagerly*—trusting Liam and the way he leads me to offer him the respect of kneeling for him. *He has earned every bit of my submission.*

"Such a good girl," he croons, walking through the doorway. Slipping one finger under my chin, he lifts my gaze from the floor up to him. He runs his thumb over my lower lip and into my mouth, massaging my tongue. I wrap my lips around it and suck as his other hand softly strokes my face. "On the bench, sweetheart."

"Again, Sir?" I tease as he takes the paddle from my hands and helps me to my feet.

He rubs his hand over the still-tiny bump. "I'm using it all I can before you grow too round to lay on your stomach."

I climb onto the spanking bench, and Liam runs his fingers over my bare skin as he wraps cuffs around both my ankles and wrists to secure me firmly to the cushion beneath my stomach. Standing before my head, he undoes his pants to make room for his rapidly growing cock, and I can't help but lick my lips.

"Always so fucking insatiable for my cock in your throat, Mrs. Evans." He nudges his pants down his hips, allowing him to pull his thick length from them. He teases, holding it just out of reach and dusting the soft skin of the thick head against my lips. Sticking out my tongue, I twirl it around the tip, and he gives me what I want. He presses over my lips, past my tongue, and down my throat with a guttural groan. "I fool myself every time I think *I'm* in charge."

I smile around his cock, and he slowly slides himself from my mouth. Bending over, he replaces the sudden void in my mouth with his tongue, kissing me fiercely.

He walks the length of the bench and rubs his hand over my ass cheeks. I delightedly moan as he places a barrage of light spanks over my skin, all delicate enough to barely cause my pale skin to pinken. When he stops, I softly beg, "More, Sir."

Liam gives me exactly what I want. He lands a palm and then another in firm strikes, the burn radiating across my skin and sending flutters straight to my core. He runs his fingers along the length of my pussy and groans. "The more it hurts, the wetter my dirty girl gets."

He lifts the paddle from the small table beside us. "You're going to be fucking soaked by the time I sink into you." Rubbing the wood over my warm, red skin, Liam instructs, "You're going to take six. Each will be harder than the last. You will count each of them. And when you're done, you're going to thank me. Understood?"

"Yes, Sir," I answer, unable to hide the anticipation in my voice. Liam swings the paddle, and it hits with a thud. "One."

"Two," I grunt when it slaps against my other cheek. Holding my breath when he swings again, I yelp, "Three!"

"Don't hold your breath. Breathe into the pain, sweetheart," Liam reminds me, tenderly rubbing over the fresh mark. "Three more."

"Four!" I barely finish calling the number when the pain of the fifth flares over my ass and through my pussy. "F...Five!"

"Last one, *mo mhuirnín*," Liam pulls back the paddle. The final swing cracks around the room as the thud reverberates through my body.

"Six!" I shout. Liam tosses the paddle to the floor and slides into me with ease. "Thank you, Sir." My gratitude is more of a grunt than words.

He takes me slowly, rubbing over the sensitive skin of my backside.

"Are you happy?" he asks, his voice soft as he pulls at the restraint around my ankle.

"I might be crying, Sir, but I've never been happier."

"Good." He slides from me, undoes the cuff and begins to work the other. "Because with or without the cuffs, you're stuck with me forever." He frees me from all the restraints and pulls me from the bench. Taking a seat in the nearby chair, he lifts me into his lap and over his cock. His hands slide along my back, pulling me flush to him as I slide down his length.

There's an unspoken promise in the way he holds me, a vow deeper than the ones from our wedding day. His lips capture mine, and he kisses me. His tongue sweeps around my mouth as though we have all the time in the world to enjoy each other. It's a kiss that tells of everything he feels for me and that I feel for him.

Losing my breath in him, I pull back for a moment. He strokes my face as I smile down at him. My heart full, I whisper, "Forever sounds perfect.... With the cuffs."

ACKNOWLEDGMENTS

First, I would like to thank my husband. Thank you for being the man who picked up my broken pieces and made me whole again.

Thank you to my readers, amazing street team and ARC team. There are not words to express how much your love and support means to me.

Thank you Amanda for all the help behind the scenes and the late night plot talks. And of course for the many shirtless men you send me for motivation—it's a selfless job, but someone has to do it.

And, as always, to Katie. Thank you for simply being you.

ALSO BY J.L. QUICK

THE MEN OF CLUB TRISKELION SERIES

- Owned
- Bound
- Primal
- Shared (Coming April 2025)
- Daddy (Coming May 2025)

THE SAVAGELY DEPRAVED SERIES

- Dark Devils
- Family Ties
- Wicked Love
- Brutal Bond

THE BOTTICELLI BROTHERHOOD SERIES

- Sold to the Syndicate
- Capo Dei Capi's Daughter
- Indebted to the Enemy
- Falling for the Mafia Dom

THE MARCANO MOGULS SERIES

- Tryst
- Crave
- Intern
- Savage

FOLLOW ME

Join my Facebook group, J.L. Quick's Good Little Readers, to get first glimpses at covers, works in progress, chapter teasers of new releases, and more!

Want to follow me on Instagram or TikTok? Check out my online store for swag and signed books? Or maybe just join my newsletter?

The QR code above has links to all of those and more too!

9 798999 271140